"Are you hurt?"

Sitting back, she shook her head. *"Nay."*

"What happened to spook your horse?"

Noah watched her pull herself together enough to stiffen. "Not my horse," she replied. "Not my buggy."

She met his gaze head-on, and he felt a jolt. She had lovely warm brown eyes, but her pallor was sickly, and he saw that she trembled. "I'm sorry," he said, not really knowing for what. "Are you cold?" He stood back and took off his coat, placing it over her shoulders and around her. "You are shaking."

She released a solid breath. "I could have been killed. You saved me. *Danki.*" A shy smile lit up her face, and in that moment he felt his pulse quicken as he noticed every little detail about her, the warmth of her golden-brown eyes, the whiteness of her smooth skin, the glimpse of her white *kapp.*

"You're Charlotte's kin, Rachel?" Noah asked. "And you are a schoolteacher," he said. "At our Happiness school?"

Rachel studied him and nodded. *"Ja."*

"Welcome to Lancaster County."

REBECCA KERTZ

has lived in rural Delaware since she was a young newlywed. First introduced into the Amish world when her husband took a job with an Amish construction crew, she took joy in watching the Amish job-foreman's children at play and in swapping recipes with his wife. Rebecca resides happily with her husband and dog. She has a strong faith in God and feels blessed to have family nearby. She enjoys visiting Lancaster County, the setting for her Amish stories. When not writing or vacationing with her extended family, she enjoys reading and doing crafts.

Noah's Sweetheart

Rebecca Kertz

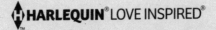
HARLEQUIN® LOVE INSPIRED®

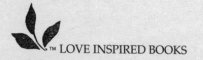
™ LOVE INSPIRED BOOKS

Recycling programs
for this product may
not exist in your area.

ISBN-13: 978-0-373-87825-3

NOAH'S SWEETHEART

Copyright © 2013 by Rebecca Kertz

This edition published by arrangement with Love Inspired Books.

® and TM are trademarks of Love Inspired Books, used under license.
Trademarks indicated with ® are registered in the United States
Patent and Trademark Office, the Canadian Trade Marks Office and in other
countries.

www.LoveInspiredBooks.com

Printed in U.S.A.

And now, Lord, what wait I for? My hope is in thee.
—*Psalms* 39:7

For Judith, with love

Chapter One

Spring...Lancaster County, Pennsylvania

Rachel Hostetler watched as Aaron Troyer took her small black valise and loaded it into the carriage.

"If you'll wait in the buggy, Rachel, my sister Martha will soon join you."

"*Danki,* Aaron." Securing the ties of her Sunday-best black bonnet, Rachel nervously chewed on her lower lip.

"Don't worry," he said. "Martha don't take up much room."

"I'm sure she doesn't." Rachel felt her stomach tighten with trepidation. It wasn't the size of Martha that concerned her. It was the type of carriage. The only vehicle available to take her from Lancaster to Happiness was this small single bench-seat buggy, the same type used for courting by the Old Order Amish. Back in Ohio, she'd ridden frequently with Abraham Beiler in a similar buggy when he was walking out with her... until the accident over a year ago that had changed her life forever.

She hadn't ridden in an open courting buggy since,

preferring the safety of her family's enclosed carriage. She didn't want to ride in one now, but it seemed that she had no choice. It was the only way for her to get to the village of Happiness and her new position as schoolteacher there.

Without thought, she slipped her hand inside her black traveling cape to touch a protective hand to her midsection. Some things just couldn't be forgotten, no matter how hard she tried. But scared or not, she'd just have to do it. It wouldn't do to start off here in this new place being a coward.

The horse shifted restlessly; Rachel gasped and retreated a few steps. *Don't be a goose,* she told herself. The bay looked like a perfectly sensible animal. But she couldn't help offering a silent prayer.

"Please, Lord, protect me from all evil," she whispered. *No matter what form evil takes.*

She stared at the buggy, took a deep breath, grabbed hold of the side and climbed on board.

"It's nice of you to drive us to town, Noah." Charlotte King smiled at her neighbor and childhood friend. "*Mam* needs more flour and cinnamon for tomorrow's baking, and *Dat* is too busy repairing the windmill to take me."

Noah nodded. "I know your *dat* is busy, Charlotte. I enjoy going to town. 'Tis no inconvenience to take you."

"And me?" Charlotte's little brother piped up.

"*Ja,* Joshua. Nice to have you along as well." He reached back and tugged the boy's straw hat down over his eyes, and Joshua giggled.

The spring sunshine felt warm against Noah's face as he steered the wagon along the blacktop road toward Bird-in-Hand. The surrounding farmland was beautiful, with spring growth in various stages. Songbirds filled the air with nature's music, and the scent of the earth permeated from the surrounding farms. Only once did the roar of a big truck that passed the buggy, blowing black from its exhaust pipes, drown out the quiet of the fields.

It was a good day for a drive; the fact that the day was to be spent in Charlotte's company only made it better. They'd be running errands for his father as well as Charlotte's mother. When Samuel Lapp had heard that Noah would be taking Charlotte to Miller's Store, he'd provided his son with his own list. He would have made the trip in a day or two himself, Samuel Lapp had told Noah, but since Noah was going now…

The three young people chatted easily as they enjoyed the ride. Spying a familiar face behind a plow, Noah lifted a hand in greeting to Abram Peachy, a member of their church.

"Nice morning for plowing, Abram. See you got an early start."

The man nodded. "Hope the weather holds out until we're done planting." His eyes focused briefly on Charlotte before shifting back to Noah beside her. "Morning, Charlotte," he said.

"Morning, Abram," Charlotte called. "How are the children?"

The widower's gaze softened. "They are doing well. 'Tis nice of you to ask."

"We're going to town!" Joshua said. "We're going to get ice cream!"

"Joshua!" Charlotte scolded with a quick look at Noah.

"I like ice cream," the boy insisted.

"You're not to pester Noah for ice cream every time

we ride into town with him," Charlotte warned. "Last time was a special treat." And to Noah, she said, "You'll spoil him rotten."

Noah winked at Joshua. "We men have to stick together, *ja?*"

Joshua giggled again and slid back on the bench seat. *"Ja."* With an impish grin at his sister, he began tapping his shoes against the floor.

"Sometimes I think you're no older than he is," Charlotte teased.

"But you like me anyway." Noah grinned at Charlotte, who couldn't help grinning back. "We're going for ice cream," he told Abram. "You have a *gut* day now."

The older man waved and then slapped the reins over the horse's back. The big Belgian walked on, and the plow cut a deep furrow in the rich, dark earth.

"A good farm, he has," Charlotte said.

"And a good farmer. A pity Abram lost his wife so young."

"God's will is sometimes hard to understand," Charlotte agreed.

It was easy to drive the wagon through the countryside. As they approached town, the number of cars on the road increased, and Noah had to handle the wagon more carefully. This area of Lancaster County invited tourists, who often didn't realize the danger of passing a horse and carriage at a great rate of speed. Fortunately, on this day, the cars they encountered slowed down appropriately. Perhaps it was the warmth of the spring day that had captured everyone's fancy on this Tuesday. Whatever the reason, Noah was able to relax and enjoy the ride and Charlotte and Joshua's company.

They bought their supplies in several small shops and then drove along the stretch of road from Miller's Store toward the village of Intercourse, where they would enjoy their ice cream. Joshua could barely contain himself; he was so excited to eat his favorite treat. Charlotte gently reprimanded her younger brother, instructing him to be still.

A dog barked ahead. A horse whinnied and then snorted. Noah heard a high-pitched scream as he saw a spooked horse rear back before bolting at a dead run in their direction. He caught sight of a woman's pale face under a bonnet as the open four-wheeled buggy came barreling down the road. He felt a thundering in his chest as he immediately saw the danger she was in.

"Charlotte, take the reins!" he said as he pulled his wagon off the road.

"Noah!" Charlotte exclaimed with alarm as Noah bounded from the wagon. "Be careful!"

But he was already running out to try and stop the panicked horse before the buggy overturned. Fear lodged in his throat at the glimpse of the terrified young Amish woman who sat in the buggy, clutching one side with white-knuckled fingers.

The horse raced closer, its ironclad hooves pounding the road. Noah shifted right, out of its path, at the last moment and then jumped to grab the animal's harness. He cried out with triumph as he got a firm handhold. *Please, Lord, give me strength!* He fought to hold on as the horse continued its runaway pace. Struggling not to become entangled in the gear, he levered himself onto the horse, gripping its sides with his legs to hold on to his seat.

The animal neighed in angry protest. Heart pounding, Noah leaned low against the horse's neck to grab hold of the reins. Successful, he straightened, pulling back on the leather straps.

"Whoa!" he called. *"Schtupp!"* He applied pressure slowly but firmly. The horse jerked and fought before breaking into a trot and finally a walk as he continued to murmur soothingly. "Gently. Take it slow, now. *Gut* boy!"

At last, the carriage rolled to a stop, still upright, as the animal finally obeyed the command, and Noah felt a sudden rush of relief. Once the horse was calm, he turned to check on the buggy's terrified passenger.

"Are you hurt?" he asked.

She gasped for breath, unable to answer. He saw only the top of her black bonnet as she bent forward, hugging herself with her arms.

He climbed down from the horse carefully, patting the animal's neck, speaking to it softly, reassuringly.

"Noah, you could have been killed." A man ran up to help Noah. He took hold of the horse's bridle, freeing Noah from the task.

"Danki, William," Noah said, recognizing a neighbor and fellow church member, William Mast. He didn't want to think about what could have happened if things hadn't gone his way.

With growing concern, he approached the occupant in the buggy, stopping at her side. "Are you hurt?" he repeated softly.

Sitting back, she shook her head. *"Nay."*

"What happened to spook your horse?"

He watched her pull herself together enough to stiffen. "Not my horse," she replied. "Not my buggy."

She met his gaze head-on, and he felt a jolt. She had lovely dark eyes, but her pallor was sickly, and he saw that she trembled. "I'm sorry," he said, not really knowing for what. "Are you cold?" He stood back and took off his coat, placing it over her shoulders and around her. "You are shaking."

She released a solid breath. "I could have been killed. You saved me. *Danki*." A shy smile lit up her face, and in that moment he felt his pulse quicken as he noticed every little detail about her…the warmth of her chocolate-brown gaze, the whiteness of her smooth skin, her small nose…the rosy pink of her lips…the glimpse of her white *kapp* beneath her black traveling bonnet. The sweep of hair from a center part across her forehead was dark. She wore a black cape over a dress of spring green.

"I was happy to help." He offered his hand to help the woman alight from the buggy. He sensed her hesitation for only a moment, and then he felt the warmth of her fingertips as she accepted his assistance.

"Rachel!" Aaron Troyer approached at a run. He nodded at William, who gave possession of the horse's bridle to its owner. The animal's sides were caked with sweat, and it was trembling all over.

"Are you all right?" Aaron asked Rachel as he ran his hand over the horse's neck and murmured soothingly to it.

"I am fine, Aaron. Thanks to—"

"Noah," Noah supplied. "Noah Lapp."

"Noah," Aaron said, out of breath. "I'm grateful." Then to the woman he said, "I didn't realize that Josef would be so easily scared. My brother meant for you and Martha to take Daisy."

"Is Josef all right?" She appeared concerned.

"*Ja,* with some care, he will be fine."

"Noah! Noah! Are you hurt?" Charlotte called out from the wagon seat. "*You could have been killed!* When I saw you jump onto that horse, I was afraid you'd fall and be crushed—" She had steered the wagon to within yards from where the buggy had come to a full stop.

"You doubt my ability with horses?" he teased. Upon seeing her expression, he sobered. "I'm fine, Charlotte."

Charlotte's gaze settled on the woman standing next to the buggy and her eyes widened. "*Rachel?* Rachel Hostetler?"

The woman seemed to search her memory before her features brightened. "Charlotte!" she exclaimed. "I am surprised that you got my message so quickly."

"We didn't." Charlotte climbed down from the wagon. "We were in town to pick up supplies for *Mam* and Noah's *vadder*. We didn't expect you to arrive until tomorrow."

"The English driver my family hired had to leave a day earlier. He had a family emergency and apologized that he couldn't drive me directly to Happiness. He left me at Troyers' Buggy Excursions. I called the number your *mam* sent me from a payphone while I waited for a ride."

"*Ja.*" Charlotte nodded. "Whittier's Store. They take messages for us."

Surprised, Noah watched and listened to the exchange with growing interest. The two women talked as if there was no one else around. "Charlotte?"

Charlotte looked startled as if she suddenly remembered there were others nearby, waiting for an introduction.

"Noah, this is Rachel Hostetler. She is our new *schuul* teacher—" Charlotte smiled "—and my cousin. Aaron—it seems that you have already met."

"You're Charlotte's kin?" Noah asked, pleased to learn that he'd be seeing more of her. Rachel nodded.

"And you are a schoolteacher," he said. "At our Happiness school?"

Rachel studied him and nodded. *"Ja."*

"Welcome to Lancaster County," he said. "Come. We'll take you home."

The intensity of Noah's regard captured her gaze. Feeling her cheeks heat, Rachel quickly looked away. She felt the warmth of his coat and, embarrassed, she removed it and handed it back to him.

"Rachel, let's go," Charlotte urged, drawing Rachel's attention and saving her from acting foolish. "You will come with us—*ja?*"

"We're going for ice cream," Joshua said.

"I don't know now, Joshua," his sister said. "Rachel has had a terrible fright. She may want to go straight home."

Rachel studied the young boy seated in the back of the wagon. "You're Joshua—and such a big boy! I'm your cousin Rachel. We've never met. The last time I saw your sister was years ago, when we were eleven and twelve, I think." She looked to Charlotte, who nodded.

"We're not going for ice cream?" Young Joshua looked crestfallen.

"No, I think I'd like to have ice cream," Rachel said, and then asked Joshua, "What kinds can we choose from?"

She did feel a bit shaky, she realized, as Joshua began to list the many flavors of ice cream available, but she didn't mind stopping for the treat first. It might help to put away the thought of what could have happened if not for the sudden appearance of Noah Lapp.

Rachel sensed the intensity of her rescuer's look, but

refused to meet his gaze. She felt as though she was still wrapped in the warmth of his coat.

"Let's go, then," Noah said quietly. "I'll get your bag."

Only then did she glance his way. His soft, quick smile in her direction did odd things to her insides.

"Are you certain, Rachel?" Charlotte asked.

She nodded at her cousin. "I have the Lord to thank for my safety. The Lord and your friend Noah Lapp."

"I'm so glad that *Mam* needed some things in town or we may not have been here when…"

Rachel shuddered.

"I'm sorry, Rachel," Aaron Troyer said.

"No harm done," Rachel assured him with a half smile. "I'm fine."

"Here's your money. Next time you need a ride, there will be no charge." After Rachel thanked him properly, Aaron left, leaving her alone with her cousins. With Rachel's bag in hand, Noah stopped to speak with Aaron.

"Are you truly all right, Rachel?" Charlotte asked. "I can't believe this happened to you. I can only imagine how you must have felt with the memory of that awful accident last year."

Rachel still felt shaken. "It was a terrible time."

"Ja," Charlotte agreed as they made their way toward the wagon on the side of the road. *"Mam* and *Dat* will be happy to see you. You'll be staying at the house until the cottage near the *schuulhaus* is finished."

"I will like that." Rachel breathed deeply in an attempt to calm her fear as she climbed onto the wagon.

"You have nothing to be afraid of, Rachel," Charlotte told her. "Noah is a *gut* driver."

Rachel nodded. "I know." She glanced in his direction.

The Lord was watching over her. He hadn't abandoned her so far from home. He'd sent her help in the form of Noah Lapp…from Happiness, Pennsylvania. What more could she ask for?

Chapter Two

The aroma of baking bread drew Rachel from the bedroom, which she shared with her cousins Charlotte and Nancy. She had overslept. Last night her sleep had been fraught with memories of the buggy accident that she'd been involved in a year ago, the near accident yesterday…and her unforgettable first encounter with Noah Lapp.

She felt terrible that she hadn't awakened earlier to help with the chores. Her relatives had been kind enough to provide a place for her; earning her keep was the least she could do.

The delicious smell grew stronger and mingled with the tantalizing scents of pies and biscuits as she descended the stairs and neared the kitchen. The warmth from the oven filled the room, surrounding her as she entered, making her feel instantly at ease, taking away some of the feeling of being far from home.

Charlotte, Nancy and Aunt Mae were gathered around the flour-dusted kitchen table, kneading dough and assembling pies. There was a streak of flour across Nancy's cheek and a dusting down the front of Charlotte's apron. Tendrils of hair had escaped from beneath their black *kapps* and their cheeks were flushed from the heat of the oven, but they didn't seem to notice or care, so intent were they on the tasks at hand. Nancy looked a lot like her older sister, but her hair was brown whereas Charlotte's was golden. Both had pretty blue eyes and ready grins.

Aunt Mae looked spotless. She wore a white *kapp* and her light brown hair in a bun from a center part that was drawn back more severely than Nancy's and Charlotte's. But there was a softness about Mae's expression that told Rachel how much her aunt enjoyed working with her daughters. As the King women worked, they chatted happily, giggling at something Nancy and then Charlotte said.

Rachel felt her heart lighten at their laughter as she approached.

After setting a layer of crust on the bottom of a pie pan, Charlotte looked up and saw her. "Rachel. *Gut* morning."

Rachel smiled. "*Gut* morning. May I help?" she asked.

"You're up," Aunt Mae said with satisfaction. "*Ja,* you can help."

"You didn't sleep well," Charlotte said, her gaze sharp as she studied her cousin.

"I'm sorry I overslept."

"You needed your rest," her aunt said. "Would you like breakfast?"

"I'd rather help with the baking."

Grinning, Charlotte and Nancy made room at the table for Rachel. "Here, Rachel," Nancy invited. "You can work here."

Rachel slid between her cousins, grabbed a bowl of

dough, and without instruction began to roll and cut out strips to make lattice for a strawberry pie that Charlotte was assembling. Working in the kitchen, she felt instantly at home.

"It's kind of you to have me." She smiled at her cousins. "I appreciate your sharing."

"We don't mind," Charlotte said. "We are family."

"There is plenty of room," Nancy agreed. "You are comfortable?"

"*Ja*. The bed is *gut*. Yesterday it was a long journey from Millersburg to Lancaster."

"It is a long way. It has been many years since I have visited my brother's family," Aunt Mae agreed. "Your driver? He is a *gut* man?"

"*Ja*, Aunt Mae, he is from Ohio, too, and has family in Lancaster County. We had to leave early, as his brother-in-law is ill and his sister needed help."

"Family is important. I am glad you had a driver who understands that." She glanced at Rachel's handiwork as she kneaded and rolled out pie dough. "Nice work. Your *mudder*, if I recall correctly, was a *gut* cook, but she does not enjoy it in the kitchen much. Who taught you to cook?"

"*Grossmudder*. She loved to bake and insisted I help whenever it was baking day." Rachel had enjoyed cooking and baking with her grandmother. *Grossmudder* had been a perfectionist when it came to her cakes, biscuits and pies, and she had instilled that trait in her eldest granddaughter. And Aunt Mae was right: her *mudder* did not like to cook, but she took care of her family, as a good wife should. Rachel and her siblings always ate well. But it was *Grossmudder* who shared her love of cooking and baking with her granddaughter, imparting a sense of understanding that family and good food went hand in hand.

Rachel began to assemble the pie lattice, placing each dough strip carefully over the filling, spacing each evenly in a lovely woven pattern. When she was done, she stood back to eye her handiwork. "Bread, biscuits and pies," she said with a smile. "Are we having company? Or are these all for family?"

Nancy spoke up. "*Nay.* We sell baked goods to a new shop in Kitchen Kettle Village. We bring them pies at least once or twice a week. Our pies sell well, and the owner is pleased to have them."

"The bread, too? It smells delicious."

Aunt Mae grinned. "The bread is for dinner this evening."

Rachel grinned with pleasure. "I can almost taste it now."

An hour later, Rachel had rolled out dough enough for three pies, made a filling for one crust, cut out biscuits and stirred the ingredients of an upside-down chocolate cake into a pan. The smell of all this good food made her stomach growl.

Charlotte chuckled. "I think you should take time for breakfast."

Her stomach protesting loudly again, Rachel said, "*Ja.* I think you're right."

"Fresh biscuits out of the oven?" Aunt Mae asked.

Rachel's mouth watered. "*Ja.* A fresh biscuit sounds *gut!*"

She ate her biscuit and sipped from her cup of tea.

"Would you like another, Rachel? Or would you like eggs and bacon?"

"*Danki,* but no, Aunt Mae. It's too late for more than

this." She rose with plate in hand to wash it in the dish basin.

Aunt Mae left the house to take Uncle Amos something to drink. Rachel's uncle was working in the fields. The day was again lovely but a little warmer, and Amos would want something to quench his thirst.

As she dried her clean plate, Rachel heard a knock resound loudly on the outside door. She couldn't see who it was as she put away the dish and hung the dish towel over the drying rack.

"Noah!" she heard Nancy exclaim, and Rachel felt her stomach flutter.

"It's nice to see you, Noah," Charlotte said cheerfully. "Would you like a biscuit or piece of pie?"

"I appreciate the offer, but no, Charlotte. After helping *Dat* early in the fields, I ate a huge breakfast."

Rachel heard every word spoken between her cousins and Noah Lapp, but she didn't turn around. With the warmth she felt since Noah's arrival, she knew her cheeks would be blazing red. Besides, he had come to visit with Charlotte, surely. Although both had behaved in the most appropriate manner in town, it seemed clear to Rachel that Charlotte and Noah were sweet on each other.

"*Gut* morning, Rachel." Suddenly Noah was next to her, overwhelming her with his presence. "Are you settling in nicely?"

Forced to meet his regard, she nodded. "*Ja.* My uncle and his family have made me most welcome." He smelled and looked nice, she thought as he turned to speak with Nancy. He must have bathed after working in the fields, for his shirt was clean, as were the dark triblend denim pants that he wore. She tried not to notice the way his suspenders fit over his shoulders. He had a firm jaw and a ready smile. His golden-brown eyes sparkled. His sandy-brown hair looked neatly combed beneath his banded straw hat.

She recalled suddenly how he'd looked yesterday after he'd rescued her: tall, thin but strong enough to leap onto the back of a galloping horse and hold on. He had lost his hat during his wild ride when he'd leaned low for the reins. His hair had become tousled and windswept during his efforts to take control of the run-away horse and buggy. She recalled how her heart had hammered and the relief she'd felt when he'd straightened, triumphant.

Watching him now, she felt the back of her neck tingle. What was wrong with her? *Abraham Beiler. Noah Lapp.* She frowned. Was one man any different from another? She was here as a schoolteacher. She would be content with teaching children other than her own.

Startled by her own thoughts, she glanced to see if anyone was watching her. Her gaze encountered her cousin Nancy, who rewarded her with a little smile.

"Rachel?" Noah's voice brought her attention back to him.

"I can't thank you enough for coming to my rescue."

"It was my pleasure." Noah smiled. Rachel looked well and content…and extremely appealing with flour on her nose and a dusting across the front of her apron. It was good to see that she suffered no lasting effects of her frightening experience the previous day.

"Noah!" Aunt Mae exclaimed as she came in from outside. "I thought I saw you from across the yard."

He reluctantly drew his attention away from Rachel to grin at her aunt. "*Gut* morning, Aunt Mae. I thought to take Rachel over to see the new *schuulhaus.*"

"That is a wonderful idea, Noah." Aunt Mae appeared delighted.

"What do you think, Rachel?" Noah asked. "Would you like to see your new *schuul?*"

"Noah and his brothers have worked hard to fix it up for you," Charlotte said.

"That was nice of you, Noah," Rachel said. "*Ja,* I would like to see the *schuulhaus.*"

"It is not far," Nancy said. "It's just off our property and down the road a little ways between our land and the farm belonging to Noah's family."

"Charlotte," Aunt Mae said, "you can go with them. Nancy can finish these pies on her own."

"Are you sure you do not want us to stay and finish?" Rachel asked.

Aunt Mae smiled. "We will be fine. Go and see where you'll be spending a lot of your time soon."

Rachel grinned. "I will enjoy this." To Noah, she said, "I will be with you in a minute. Just let me get cleaned up."

The relief he felt when she agreed to come made Noah realize just how eager he was to show her the *schuul.*

Charlotte and Rachel went upstairs to change their aprons and wash their hands and faces of baking dust. Rachel was the first one downstairs and out the door.

When she stepped outside, she noticed the buggy parked in the yard. It was an enclosed family buggy with a gray roof. Seeing it, she sighed with relief. Two mishaps in small open buggies had made her leery of riding in one again. She and Noah were alone, waiting for Charlotte to join them.

She grinned at Noah. "Nice carriage."

Noah grinned back, pleased by her response. "I

thought after that little accident yesterday that you'd prefer riding in this." Her smile made him feel good inside.

"Danki," she said.

Charlotte soon appeared, and she climbed into the front seat next to Noah, while Rachel climbed into the back.

"And I hitched old Janey. She's twenty-five years old and you couldn't get her out of a trot if you tried." Noah clicked his tongue, slapped the reins, and the carriage took off down the dirt lane toward the main road.

Rachel sat behind Noah, aware of his straw-brimmed hat, his sandy-brown hair cut in the bowl-cap style that all the Old Order Amish men wore.

Charlotte turned around to smile at her. "I think you will like the schoolhouse. Samuel Lapp and his sons built a new one, large enough for all of the school-aged children in our church district. The Lapp men are good carpenters. Noah is the best, after his *vadder*."

"How many brothers do you have, Noah?" Rachel asked.

"Six," he said with his eyes still on the road. They had come to the end of the lane and he steered the buggy left onto the paved street. "Jedidiah is the eldest, then I am next." He turned his head to flash her a quick smile before his gaze returned to the road.

"The Samuel Lapps include Samuel's seven sons and one daughter," Charlotte said. "Hannah is only six months old."

"You will meet them all on Sunday," Noah said. "It's visiting Sunday, and some of our friends will meet at our family farm."

The clip-clop of the horse's hooves was the only sound in the buggy for a time, allowing Rachel to digest what she had learned. Noah pulled the carriage off the blacktop and onto a dirt drive that ran next to a white building with a front porch.

"The *schuulhaus*," Charlotte announced.

Charlotte got out on the right side of the vehicle. Noah climbed down and offered his hand to Rachel. "Welcome to your new *schuul*."

Conscious of Noah's relationship with Charlotte, Rachel smiled as she ignored his hand and stepped out of the buggy on her own. She studied the building with excitement. This was her school! Soon, it would be filled with her students!

"It is very nice," she said sincerely. "The nicest *schuulhaus* I've ever seen."

Noah looked pleased. "Let's go inside."

They heard hammering as they approached. "Jedidiah or *Dat* is finishing up," Noah said.

The door swung in easily, and Rachel and Charlotte followed Noah inside. An older man with hammer in hand was bent low over a floorboard. *"Dat,"* Noah greeted.

"Noah, you have brought our new schoolteacher."

"Ja, this is Rachel Hostetler," Noah introduced. "Rachel, my *vadder*—Samuel Lapp."

Rachel nodded. "It is nice to meet you. You have done a *gut* job with this school. I am happy to see it."

Samuel's eyes sparkled in a face that was an older version of his son Noah's, except for the beard that edged his chin. As in Rachel's Ohio Amish community, married men wore beards along their chins, but not on their upper lips. "Come in. Come in and look about. There is much for you to see."

The interior of the one-room schoolhouse was white and smelled of fresh paint and newly varnished wood.

Someone had been thoughtful enough to hang posters of the alphabet printed on lines like those on primary writing paper. There were also numbers from one to ten. Beside the schoolroom door, there were built-in glass-fronted cabinets. The community or school board had been kind enough to fill the shelves with books.

Noah and Charlotte talked with Samuel while Rachel wandered about, studying her surroundings.

What captured her heart the most were the rows of student desks—five rows of eight, all newly crafted, stained and varnished and ready for use. Her heart gave a little leap as Rachel saw the teacher's desk at the front of the class. It was a beautiful piece of furniture, made with care. She approached the desk and ran her fingers over the smooth, varnished surface.

"You like the desk?" Noah asked, suddenly beside her.

Rachel had sensed him instantly. She glanced over at him and nodded. "It is a wonderful desk." Her gaze flashed briefly to the other side of the room and Charlotte, who was grinning at something Noah's father had said. Her attention returned to Noah standing next to her. "It is beautiful."

"I'm glad you like it. I made it."

"You did?" She was impressed. "You are not only a carpenter but a cabinetmaker as well?"

Noah shrugged, downplaying his enjoyment of creating something wonderful from a few blocks of wood, of running his fingers over the smooth, polished surface as he eyed the finished product. "I like making furniture. My *grossdaddi* makes wonderful furniture. Many come from miles around to buy his chairs and tables."

"A fine craft he has—as do you." She awarded him a smile. "I will enjoy the desk."

Noah felt a rush of pleasure. He didn't know what it was about Rachel, but he was feeling things he'd never felt before. He became aware of a sudden desire to confide in her, to tell her about his dream of opening his own furniture shop someday. "Rachel—" he began, but stopped at Charlotte's approach.

"Do you like the new school?" Charlotte asked.

"*Ja.* It will be a good place to teach the children." She eyed the number of desks. "Are there that many children who will attend school?"

Charlotte chuckled. "Not yet, but the bishop wanted to make sure that there would be room for more in the future."

Rachel felt a sigh of relief. "There are forty desks."

"*Ja,* but only thirty-one children," Charlotte said and then laughed when she saw her cousin's astonished expression.

"It is a good thing we have the room, then," Rachel agreed. *Thirty-one children!* It was going to be an interesting school year, she thought.

"Rachel," Noah said. "Let us show you where your house will be."

She turned to Noah's father. "It is a wonderful *schuulhaus,* Samuel. I appreciate all that you and your sons have done."

Samuel graciously accepted Rachel's thanks. "I will see you on Sunday, Rachel, if not before."

"*Ja,*" she said with a nod. "I will see you on Sunday."

Then she followed Noah and Charlotte outside and they headed farther down the dirt lane in the opposite direction from where they had parked the buggy.

Chapter Three

They walked in silence; the only sounds were the crunch of their shoes against dirt and gravel, the distant tapping of a hammer coming from inside the school, and the sweet chirping of a robin redbreast.

Rachel, pleased with the schoolhouse, could hardly wait to see where she would live as the teacher. She wasn't expecting anything fancy. She needed only the basics to make a home. Whatever her family district provided, she'd be grateful for.

They'd not gone far when she'd spied the building. She gasped in wonder. It was a small cottage, slightly bigger than the schoolhouse with white siding, working dark blue window shutters and a matching blue door. She couldn't help the silly grin that spread to her lips. "This is the teacher's house?"

"Ja." Noah gazed at her with a smile. "Do you like it?"

Rachel nodded, still grinning. "It is lovely." It was unusual for the school board to build a house for the teacher. Usually the teacher was selected from among the members of the community, but Rachel was from

Millersburg, Ohio, far away. Was that why she would have her own house as long as she continued to teach here? *Lord, thank You for Your blessings.*

"It will be the right size for you, *ja?*" Charlotte said. Rachel saw that her cousin looked happy for her.

"It is perfect," Rachel agreed. She was eager to get a closer look. "Is it safe to go inside?"

"*Ja,* we can go in and look around," Noah said, "but I don't want you to be disappointed. The outside is finished, but the inside is not."

As she stepped into the interior of the house, Rachel felt a sense of home. There were only wooden studs where the walls would be, but she could see the size of each room and the opening of each doorway. Her imagination finished the rest for her.

"I'm sorry it is not done yet," Noah apologized.

Rachel met his gaze. "I'm not," she said sincerely. "I will enjoy watching each stage of construction." And she could help. She wasn't afraid of hard work.

"*Dat* thought it would be best to get the *schuulhaus* finished first," Noah said as he led the way to the back of the house and into a room that, Rachel decided after judging its size, must be the kitchen. "The old *schuulhaus* burned to the ground last summer." He waited for Charlotte, who had stopped to gaze out a window, to catch up. Once she joined them, he continued on. "We will work on the house next. We have been busy planting, but we will do our best to get it done for you soon."

"I'm grateful." Rachel rewarded her cousin with a smile. "As long as Charlotte doesn't mind sharing, I don't mind waiting for the house. It is fun to spend time with my Lancaster County family."

Charlotte grinned back. "And we like having our cousin stay with us."

Noah gave the two cousins a guided tour and then showed them the yard out back. "You will be able to plant a vegetable garden here. There is plenty of room. I'll be glad to come over and plow an area for you. And look—" He pointed to two spreading, flowering trees with white blossoms, not far from the back door. "You will have your own apple trees. They are Braeburn."

"A *gut* all-around apple." Rachel went to examine them more closely. "I will enjoy having apple trees. I can share fresh, crisp apples with the *kinner.* They can eat them during recess."

"And you can make apple pies," Charlotte said. "You make delicious pies."

"I would like a piece of Rachel's apple pie," Noah told Charlotte in a low, teasing undertone.

"I heard that!" Rachel's voice held a hint of laughter.

"You would keep pie from one of the builders of your new house?" Noah said, feigning sadness.

Rachel sighed…loudly. "All right. You can have a piece of my apple pie." Noah's face lit up with eagerness, and Rachel caught her breath at how handsome he looked. Fighting the feeling, she added, "As long as you get my house done before apple season."

"It will be done in a month," Noah promised.

"If he says it will be done, it will be done," Charlotte said when Rachel was skeptical. "The Lapp men are good carpenters."

"Men of many talents," Rachel said softly, thinking of Noah, recalling his skill with her rescue and the desk he'd made for the teacher.

"It is getting late," Noah said. "Aunt Mae will be wondering why I kept you so long."

"Ja," Charlotte said. "There is cooking to be done before we come on Sunday."

Rachel had almost forgotten. They would be spending time at the Lapp farm on Sunday. She would meet not only Noah's mother, but also all of his other kin. She was both terrified and excited by the prospect. Were all of the Lapp brothers as handsome as Noah?

They left the cottage, and it seemed a much shorter walk back to the buggy, where the old mare Janey waited patiently for their return. Rachel climbed into the back of the buggy, conscious of Noah waiting for her and Charlotte to be seated.

"I will be right back," Noah said and he disappeared around to the rear of the schoolhouse. He was back within minutes with two handfuls of wildflowers. Without a word, he gave Charlotte and Rachel each a small bouquet of colorful, delicate blooms.

Rachel remained silent as Charlotte thanked him profusely. The gesture was sweet and thoughtful, and she didn't know what to make of it. No doubt he'd wanted to give flowers to Charlotte but felt it'd be awkward not to give any to Rachel.

Whatever his reasons, Noah had pleased her, and Rachel tried to shut down her feelings. It wouldn't do to like Noah, who was the man in her cousin's life. It wouldn't do to get involved with any man. She had learned a hard lesson from Abraham Beiler, and she should never, ever—could never, ever—forget how awful she'd felt.

Rachel went with the Amos King women to the Lapp farm on Friday. She hadn't expected to visit so soon, but Katie Lapp had seven sons and only a baby daughter. Katie needed help getting ready for the five families who would come to visit on Sunday.

They had delivered pies to Kitchen Kettle Village on

Thursday morning. On Thursday afternoon they had baked two more cakes and four more pies. These treats were for the social.

Rachel had a pie on her lap as Aunt Mae drove the family buggy over to the Lapp farm. It didn't take long to get there. As her aunt pulled the carriage into the Lapps' barnyard, Rachel stared at the house. It was a big house, bigger than the Amos Kings' and bigger than her home back in Ohio. White with a large front porch and many windows across the second and first floors, it was a plain but beautiful structure that displayed signs of a contented life.

Her aunt and cousins alighted, and as she climbed out, Rachel was conscious of chickens clucking and running about the yard. A low mooing from the barn could only have come from the family cow. Two young Amish boys of about six or seven ran about, chasing each other, while an older boy, who looked to be eleven or twelve, carried wood from the shed with his gaze on his two younger brothers. Noah's brothers? Rachel wondered.

"John! Jacob!" Aunt Mae called. "Come say hello to your new schoolteacher." She turned to Rachel. "John is *mei kinskind.* He is your cousin Sarah's son. He is five."

Rachel blinked. "Sarah? Sarah is here?"

Aunt Mae nodded. "She and Eli live on the other side of Bird-in-Hand. They have been away to Delaware. They were due back late yesterday." She smiled as the boys approached slowly, eyeing Rachel with cautious curiosity.

Rachel hadn't realized that Sarah had had children. Sarah was the eldest of the Amos Kings. She had married when Rachel and Charlotte were young children, so it was natural that she now had one or more daughters or sons. She studied John, Sarah's son. He was a handsome boy with blond hair and brown eyes. Did he look like his *vadder* or Sarah? Rachel could barely remember what her cousin Sarah looked like.

"Rachel," her aunt said, "these boys will be your students. John, Jacob, this is your new schoolteacher. John, Rachel is also your cousin. Jacob belongs to Abram Peachy. Abram is deacon." And then to Rachel, she whispered, "and a widower." The boys had started to turn away, ready to play again.

She called after them. "Boys! What do you say to your new schoolteacher?"

"*Gut* day to you, Rachel. We are pleased to meet you." It was Jacob Peachy who spoke.

John stared at her. "What do I need school for? I like working on the farm."

"You must learn English," Rachel said, "so that you can do farm business in town."

Jacob was nodding as if he understood. "*Ja,* John. You don't want to be a bad farmer, do you?"

"I will be a *gut* farmer! I know a lot about plowing and planting…and harvesting!"

"I'm sure you do, John," his grandmother said. "But Rachel is right, it is important for you to learn things to help you someday when you are big and can take over your father's farm."

"We will both come," Jacob added.

Rachel gazed at his sweet face and thought how unfortunate it was that this poor boy had lost his mother. "I will see you in class in two months."

The boys nodded before they ran off to finish their barnyard play.

Rachel became aware of several things at once as she entered the Lapp family home. First was that the house was filled with women she didn't know. Then she saw Charlotte greet another woman warmly with a hug. She heard "Sarah" and she realized that this was the cousin she had met only once when she was barely old enough to remember.

Charlotte came back and grabbed Rachel's hand, leading her toward her older sister. "Sarah, this is cousin Rachel."

Sarah smiled. She looked so much like Aunt Mae that Rachel had to keep herself from staring. "You were young when we met."

Rachel nodded. "*Ja.* You took me for a walk to see the barn animals."

"That's right." Her eldest cousin looked surprised. "You were three."

Rachel studied her cousin's face carefully. "You have the look of your *mudder.*"

"We all do," Sarah said, referring to her sisters. She turned to softly scold a little girl who was trying to put her fingers into a freshly baked chocolate-cream pie. It was one of Rachel's pies brought from Aunt Mae's, which hadn't been put in a cool place yet. "Rose Ann!" she exclaimed. "You must not touch that pie." Seeing the little girl's face begin to crumple, Sarah bent to scoop up the child into her arms. "You can have a piece of pie when we get home." She kissed her daughter's forehead and turned back to Rachel. "This is my youngest—Rose Ann. She is three and she likes chocolate."

Little Rose Ann nodded vigorously. "Chocolate."

Rachel felt her heart melting as she stared into her little cousin's hazel eyes. Rose Ann's hair had a hint of red highlights. She was a beautiful child with an inner glow.

"Ah, pie!" Noah was suddenly near the pie, ready to do what little Rose Ann was forbidden to.

"Nay!" Rachel exclaimed. She had sensed immediately when he'd come in. "That is for Sunday. You must not touch it now—"

"Just a taste?" he asked with a look of boyish innocence, but Rachel could see the mischievous twinkle that spoiled his whole act.

"Ows!" Charlotte exclaimed. "Rachel is right. You should not be here. We are here to do women's work. You don't look like a woman to me."

Noah's face beamed. "I'm glad you noticed."

"No-ah!" Katie Lapp's sharp tone was like a shout across the room.

"Mam?" he said as his mother approached. Katie was a strikingly plain woman who would stand out no matter if she wore Amish clothing or a potato sack. Her white prayer *kapp* sat properly on her head, revealing a glimpse of sandy-brown hair, the same color as her son's.

"Doesn't Jedidiah need help moving the furniture?"

"We finished in the house, *Mam*."

"Then go check with your *vadder*. I'm sure he has something for his wild son to do." But Katie's tone had become soft, affectionate. It was clear that she loved him.

"I only wanted a piece of pie."

"Pie for Sunday," little Rose Ann said firmly.

Noah flashed the little girl a bright smile. "Right you are, then, Rosie." He lowered his voice. "We just wanted one little piece, didn't we?"

Rose Ann grinned and nodded. "Just one piece."

"I guess I had better find something to do before the pie begs me to grab a bite of it." And Noah left, taking some of the fresh air that had come in with him.

"Charlotte, he will be a handful, that one," Sarah said.

Charlotte nodded, but her eyes held warmth and something like affection…or more. "Noah Lapp is a man all to his own."

Rachel, listening to the exchange, felt a little knot form in her stomach. She had to avoid him. He was Charlotte's special friend—not hers. Something she couldn't—mustn't—forget.

She'd been amazed by Noah's ability to make a small child feel special. She had seen him come in and pour himself a glass of water from a pitcher. The last thing he'd seemed to want was a piece of chocolate-cream pie, but he had heard the exchange between little Rose Ann and her mother.

He was a special man. *No, I mustn't think about him!* She felt a twinge of guilt. There were reasons for her to forget Noah Lapp, and it was more than just his being her cousin Charlotte's friend. They might not be courting yet, but no doubt they would be soon. And wasn't that reason enough itself? The two were more than comfortable with each other. Just the way she and Abraham had been when they'd begun courting. She fought back mixed emotions. There were other reasons not to become involved with a man again—reasons she wasn't ready to ponder too deeply.

The women began to disperse to different areas of the house, where they would work to give the rooms a thorough cleaning. Katie accepted their help with silent gratitude. Rachel approached to introduce herself, and Katie placed her arm around Rachel's shoulder as she led her into the large front room.

"I have heard much about you, Rachel," Noah's mother said pleasantly. "You like the new school?"

Rachel beamed. "*Ja.* Samuel and your sons have done a *gut* job."

"You will have a lot of children in class." Katie walked through the room, checking that all was in order.

"Will I have some of your sons?"

"*Ja.* You will have Daniel and Joseph, my two youngest sons."

"I look forward to having them in school."

A baby cried from above, but was instantly silent. Katie's expression was soft. "That is Hannah, my baby daughter. She has been napping. Someone must have picked her up." She seemed unconcerned about who had seen to her daughter. Unlike the Englishers, the Amish cared for their neighbors and their community and were always willing to lend a hand.

Katie straightened a framed embroidered wallhanging. On it, the Lapp family tree was depicted. Rachel saw Katie and Samuel and all their children: Jedidiah, Noah, Jacob, Elijah, Isaac, Daniel, Joseph, and little Hannah. It was a lovely piece of stitchery.

Noah's mother studied the family tree for a moment before turning slowly to capture Rachel's gaze. "Mae and I are close, almost as close as sisters."

Rachel waited, sensing the woman had something to say.

"Rachel, I hope you can begin a new life in Happiness." She glanced back at the frame on the wall. "It is sometimes difficult to start over," she said. "Are you doing well?" Her brown eyes found and steadily held Rachel's attention.

"*Ja.* Everyone has been welcoming."

Katie smiled. "*Gut.* That is how it should be." She seemed to hesitate a moment. "You are feeling well?"

Rachel frowned, uncertain of what Katie meant. "I am fine."

"Your accident. I read about it in *The Budget*."

She must have looked upset, because Katie patted her arm. "No one knows but you, me and your aunt Mae. It is my relationship with Mae that made me understand what happened."

How much did she know? Rachel wondered fearfully.

"You spent weeks in the hospital."

Rachel nodded. "I was walking out with Abraham Beiler. We were in his courting buggy with my brother Moses as chaperone. It was winter and the road was icy. We were managing fine until a car came speeding around the bend and forced us off the road. I was on the right side and I fell into an ice-water-filled ditch. The buggy fell on top of me. Abraham and Moses were injured only slightly. I was hurt the worst."

Katie's eyes softened with sympathy. "It must have been terrible."

"*Ja.* It was a dark time, but I had the Lord to guide me until the darkness lifted." If it hadn't been for her faith in God, she would never have survived her injuries and the time that followed.

"And Abraham?" Katie waited as if she already knew but wanted to hear Rachel's version.

"He decided that I was not the girl for him. He began courting Emma Mast, my best friend, before I even got out of the hospital. They were married in September." Only six months after he'd asked to court her… and not Emma. They hadn't even waited until the time most couples married in their Ohio Amish community.

"It must have been awful for you," Katie said. "But I can see that you are well and doing fine. You are a schoolteacher and in our village of Happiness! I think you will like it here, Rachel. The Lord works in ways we can't always understand, but I have a feeling that you were meant to come here…that Happiness was God's plan for you all along."

Rachel could only nod. "Katie—"

"I will tell no one of what happened to you in Millersburg, Rachel. Your secret is safe with me." She gestured toward the door to the kitchen. "Let's have a cup of tea. If we don't stand watch, there may be no pies and cakes for Sunday. My sons are big eaters."

Relieved at the change of subject, Rachel gladly accompanied Katie Lapp into the kitchen, where two neighbor women were rearranging Sunday's desserts.

"Shall we put this in the refrigerator?" Agnes Troyer asked of Rachel's chocolate-cream pie.

"*Ja,* it will keep better," Katie said.

"I'll take it," Rachel offered, eager for a few moments alone after her heart-to-heart talk with her aunt's friend Katie. She picked up the pie and went into the other room, where a gas refrigerator and separate gas freezer were located. She opened the refrigerator door, her hands shaking slightly as she rearranged a few items to make room for the pie. When the pie had its own place, she shut the refrigerator door and leaned against it. Her heart was beating rapidly. There was a sick feeling in the pit of her stomach. She didn't like to remember the accident that had changed her life and taken away her sweetheart.

Thank You, Lord. I praise You, Lord, for all Your goodness and grace. Thank You for not allowing anyone to realize just how much the accident changed me. Thank You for being there whenever I need You.

She stood for a moment, fighting tears, reining in her emotions. Upon hearing laughter from within the kitchen, Rachel straightened. She wiped her eyes, pulled herself together and went back to rejoin the others to ask what she could do to help.

Chapter Four

Noah stood on the front porch of the Lapp family farmhouse, watching as neighbors and friends drove their horses into the yard and parked in line with the other gray family buggies. All of the male Samuel Lapps—from their father Samuel to his youngest son, Joseph—were dressed in their black Sunday best. They stood, offering greetings and handshakes as the Amish men from other households joined them on the porch, while the women bustled into the house to join Katie in the kitchen.

The Kings' gelding trotted down the lane and turned into the yard. Noah felt an odd sensation in the pit of his stomach as the family alighted from the buggy and crossed toward the house.

He nodded to Charlotte's father as Amos climbed the porch steps and joined them. "Fair weather this day," he said, and the man agreed. Conscious of the women, especially Rachel, who got out of the buggy last, he turned his attention first to little Joshua, who had run up to the house. "Have any ice cream lately?"

"Nay." Joshua scowled. His eyes suddenly lit up. "Can we go this week?"

"If there is time for a trip into town."

"Joshua!" Charlotte scolded as she climbed up the stairs. "What did I tell you about bothering Noah?"

"I wasn't bothering him." He looked up at Noah with big eyes. "Was I?"

"Nay, Joshua," Noah replied and then grinned at Charlotte. "What's that you're carrying?" he asked her. "Could it be chocolate cake?"

Charlotte's eyes twinkled. "Shoofly pie."

Noah knew the exact moment when Rachel climbed the first step of his family home. She was wearing a blue dress with black apron and cape. This day her bonnet and the prayer *kapp* covering her dark hair were both black. She was lovely, and he couldn't take his eyes off her sweet face. "And what do you have there?" he asked, casually, forcing himself to study the pie in her arms. "Another chocolate-cream pie?"

"Ja." She met his gaze but then quickly glanced away.

"I think I'd like some of that pie," he murmured softly for her ears only as she hurried past, following in her cousin's footsteps.

"That was the new schoolteacher?" Jedidiah said.

Noah narrowed his gaze on his older brother. "I thought you saw her when she came to help *Mam.*"

Jedidiah, watching the arrival of another buggy, shook his head. *"Dat* and I were finishing up at the *schuulhaus."* His attention fixed on Abram Peachy as he climbed out of his buggy and helped his five children to alight. "I heard you got your fields planted," he called to Abram.

Abram waved his children into the house. "The weather held, thanks be to God."

"You meet the new schoolteacher yet?" Jedidiah asked, and Noah glanced at his brother sharply before turning to gauge Abram's response.

"Nay," Abram said. "I hear she's a King cousin from Ohio." He seemed to exhibit only polite interest.

Noah felt himself relax. *"Ja.* Rachel Hostetler."

"Nice girl," Noah's father said.

Jedidiah elbowed his brother. "I hear you were the great rescuer the other day."

Noah shrugged. "'Twas nothing."

"Not from what my daughter tells me," Amos King said.

Abram suddenly looked interested. "Something happen in town?"

"Ja," little Joshua piped up, as he returned from inside to stand with the men. "Aaron Troyer's horse spooked, and Noah saved cousin Rachel from crashing."

Abram smiled. "From crashing what?"

Joshua pulled himself up and tugged on the bottom of his small black coat. At seven, he was a miniature version of his father. "The buggy! The horse was galloping right down the middle of the road, and he took Rachel and the buggy with him. Noah had to jump onto the horse's back while he was still running to stop him. The horse's eyes were rolled back in his head, all big and white, and he was sweaty. Aaron Troyer came running up to take care of his horse Josef and to see if Rachel hurt herself!"

Noah felt himself the object of several male gazes. He was uncomfortable with this particular discussion and being the center of attention. "It wasn't anything one of you wouldn't do."

"That's not what cousin Rachel said," Joshua replied. "She said she could have been killed if Noah hadn't come to save her."

"Ja." Abram removed his hat, pushed his hair back, and then settled his wide-brimmed black-felt hat back on his head. "Could have been. One of Obadiah Fisher's daughters out in Missouri—she got killed last summer when her horse ran away. Terrible thing for the family, and her just fifteen. Lucky for the new teacher you were there."

The Zook family arrived at that moment, putting a temporary end to the topic of conversation. As he greeted "Horseshoe Joe" Zook's wife, Miriam, Noah could feel Jedidiah watching him. He pretended not to notice, and soon Jedidiah's attention turned to the middle Zook daughter, Annie.

Five families had come to visit. The men stayed outside while the women inside readied the midday meal. Moments of the men's conversation intermingled with periods of silence, as the weather was good and there wasn't a need for talking.

"The cousin was grateful," Jedidiah said to Noah. "What does Charlotte think? Must have put a fright into her, seeing it."

"Rachel is Charlotte's first cousin. She's glad I was there to help."

Noah wondered how Rachel was getting along. She'd been here less than a week, and she must have feelings about their Happiness community.

"Charlotte is an understanding girl," his brother persisted. "Good head on her shoulders. Make some man a mighty good wife."

Noah glared at him, wondering where Jedidiah was

headed with this conversation. "And why are you telling me? Charlotte and I have known each other a long time."

"Ja," Jedidiah said, "and well you should remember this."

His older brother could be annoying at times, Noah thought. They were close in age—Jedidiah was only a year and a half older than he was. What was Jedidiah implying? That Charlotte was jealous? That he shouldn't have saved Rachel because he and Charlotte were friends?

Noah shook his head. Sometimes Jedidiah made no sense.

"He did save her!" He suddenly heard Joshua shout from across the yard. "Ask him. Better you should ask cousin Rachel! Cousin Rachel!" the little boy called as he ran from the barn toward the house, followed closely by Jacob Peachy.

The boys rushed inside before Noah could stop either one of them. The last thing he needed was for Rachel to become embarrassed by all the attention—no matter how innocently it began.

"Cousin Rachel!" Joshua cried.

Noah cringed. All he did was stop a runaway buggy. Why couldn't everyone just leave things be?

"…And the little Englisher was caught stealing a brownie from a pan cooling on Elisabeth Schrock's windowsill," Alta Hershberger was saying.

Miriam Zook's eyes widened. "What did she do?"

Alta grinned. "She gave him a piece of her mind and then handed him another brownie."

The women chuckled in response as they unwrapped the food they'd prepared previously.

"Abram's children are growing fast, like weeds,"

Mae commented as she sliced bread and arranged muffins. "Such a shame that those precious children have no *mudder* to guide them."

"Abram's doing the best he can, *Mam*," Charlotte said.

"*Ja,* daughter. But the deacon can't be all things to everyone. It's hard when there are children to raise alone and a farm to run. It's time he thought about marrying again."

"I'm sure he will when he is ready," Katie said gently. She unwrapped a plate and set it on the table. "A shame Sarah couldn't come."

"*Ja,*" Aunt Mae said. "I was sorry to hear David came down sick—"

Two young boys burst into the kitchen and stopped, the door slamming shut behind them. "Rachel! Cousin Rachel!"

"Son!" Aunt Mae scolded. "We walk, not run, into a room!"

Rachel grinned as Joshua searched the room and found her. "Little cousin, what's wrong?" She tossed each boy an apple from a bowl on the counter.

"Jacob doesn't believe that Noah saved you!" Joshua exclaimed before he took a big bite.

"Noah did save me, Jacob," Rachel said, her breath catching at the mention of Noah's name. "If he hadn't stopped the horse, the buggy could have hit someone or something, and I could have been hurt or even killed."

Jacob's eyes went big as he listened to Rachel. "Noah saved her," he said to Joshua. "And he kept Aaron Troyer's horse from maybe breaking a leg and having to be shot."

Joshua nodded vigorously, glad that his friend finally

understood. "When are we going to eat?" he asked his sister, who'd been listening with amusement.

"Soon," Charlotte said, handing each boy an apple-walnut muffin. "Go outside and be *gut* boys. We will call you when it is your time to eat."

"Would you take this to the table?" Miriam asked.

Rachel nodded. She accepted the large bowl of potato salad and carried it into the front room, where she set it down on one of several makeshift tables that had been constructed for today's visit. Her thoughts on Noah, she went to the window and peered outside. She couldn't see him at first, and she started to turn away. Then his father moved and there he was, speaking with two men she hadn't met. Noah nodded and then smiled at someone's answer. He turned toward the house as he chatted, and his gaze locked with hers briefly through the glass. Rachel quickly retreated, embarrassed at being caught staring. She hurried back to the kitchen.

"The meal is ready," Katie Lapp announced to the men outside.

The oldest men entered the house first. They sat down at a table, and then the younger men took their seats. The women had prepared the food earlier in the week. There was cold roast beef and chicken, potato salad, sweetened-and-vinegared green beans with bacon, frosted raisin bread, sweet-and-sour chow-chow, muffins, yeast rolls and coleslaw. There was an assortment of cakes and pies for dessert, including Charlotte's shoofly pie and Rachel's chocolate-cream pie.

The men ate without conversation, and when they were done, the women and children sat down to eat. Rachel enjoyed the meal, especially the sliced roast beef and potato salad with peas. Aunt Mae had made the green beans, and they were delicious.

Nancy took a second helping of her mother's dish before tasting other foods. "*Mam* makes the best sauce for her beans," she said.

Rachel smiled. "Everything is wonderful. Did you have some of Miriam's chow-chow? Sweet and sour is my favorite."

"Mine, too," Charlotte replied as she lifted a forkful of the vegetables to her mouth. "Did you see Alta Hershberger's vanilla pudding? Before the day is done, I'm going to have me a cup."

"May I have some pudding with you?" A little girl stood at Charlotte's side.

Charlotte's expression softened. "I'll call you when I'm ready to get some. I'll scoop you a cup so we can eat it together." The child looked pleased as she turned and ran back to sit with her sister and brothers. "That's Ruth Peachy," she told Rachel. "Abram's youngest."

Rachel eyed the youngest Peachy child as the little girl ate carefully, mimicking her older sister. "She's too young for my classroom."

Charlotte agreed. "She's not yet four. She's a pleasant girl. For some reason, she's taken a liking to me."

"The reason is simple," Rachel said. "You're as purehearted as she is, and you treat her nicely."

"I like her."

Rachel smiled. "I can tell you do."

Suddenly, Rachel felt the back of her neck prickle. She turned, only to encounter Noah's gaze.

Charlotte stood and approached him. "Can I get you something?"

Noah withdrew his gaze, turning his smiling attention to Charlotte. "Not unless you're cutting the pies."

Charlotte chuckled. "We'll be serving them soon,

Noah." Her eyes twinkled. "You're still hungry?" she teased.

"Only for pie or cake."

"I'll bring you a piece after we cut it," she offered.

Noah shook his head. "I'll be back to get it myself." His eyes met Rachel's briefly as he left as quickly as he'd come.

Everyone enjoyed the cakes, pies and other sweets provided by the women. Noah had come for his piece of Rachel's chocolate-cream pie, as promised. He appeared to relish every bite before he was back for more. Rachel couldn't help feeling pleased that he took so much pleasure from it. Charlotte and Ruth Peachy sat side by side with their bowls of vanilla pudding. It seemed the most natural thing when Charlotte reached over to wipe pudding off the little girl's mouth when Ruth was done. Rachel ate a tiny slice of shoofly pie and then enjoyed a small taste of Miriam Zook's butter coffee cake. Soon, with bellies full and the time growing late, families began to gather their leftovers and their youngsters to leave.

Later, only the Amos Kings and Rachel stayed behind to visit a little longer with the Samuel Lapps and to help Katie with the cleanup. As she collected dishes to bring to the kitchen, Rachel saw the older Lapp brothers begin to take apart the front-room tables. She had met all of Noah's brothers this day. They were a fine bunch of young men and boys who teased each other while they worked together as a team. Hearing them reminded her of her own three brothers back home in Millersburg, and she got misty-eyed for a few seconds. There was at least one Lapp brother close in age to each of her brothers, Moses, David and Thomas, who were all younger than she. Today would be their day for Sunday visiting, too, and it did make her feel a little better to know that, in a way, things were the same here as back in Millersburg.

The kitchen was clean, and the food was put away in Katie's refrigerator and pantry or in dishes ready for the Kings to take home. The men had gone outside to look at Samuel's new milk cow. Katie, Aunt Mae, Rachel and her cousins sat on the front porch. Katie bounced her baby daughter on her knee. Little Hannah had been happy and smiling since she'd woken from her nap and eaten. She seemed content to sit on her mother's lap and gaze at the other women.

Rachel studied the little girl and had the strongest urge to hold her. "May I?" she asked Hannah's mother.

"*Ja.* Don't be alarmed if she fusses," Katie warned as she surrendered her baby into Rachel's outstretched arms.

Baby Hannah cuddled against her without complaint. Rachel felt an overwhelming contentment as she rocked to and fro in the front-porch rocking chair, enjoying the warmth of the spring afternoon in the companionship of women she liked and respected.

Soon it was time for the Kings to return home. They didn't have far to go, but it was getting late and there would be time for the family to enjoy the rest of the day reading, playing games or just resting in the comfort of their own home. Rachel stood and handed Hannah back to her mother. To everyone's surprise, Hannah fussed a little before she settled down as Katie stood, rocking her against her shoulder.

"Good food and fine company," Aunt Mae said. "A perfect Sunday visiting."

Rachel and her cousins agreed. "*Ja,* and the weather

is fine," Nancy added. They went inside to gather their dishes and the leftovers given to them by their hostess.

"It's been a *gut* day," Rachel said as she prepared to descend the porch steps. There was no sign of the men yet, but she expected them to appear at any moment.

Katie smiled as she continued to pat her daughter's back. "I enjoyed your company." Her gaze shot past Rachel toward the barnyard. "You'll come again soon. Don't wait until next Sunday's church services to see us."

Rachel murmured agreement as she glanced back to see Samuel, her uncle Amos, Noah and three of his brothers as they stepped from the barn and started toward the house. She watched the men's approach, trying not to look too much at Noah, but it was Noah who drew her attention. When she realized that he watched her, she felt her face warm and quickly glanced away.

With a dish in hand, she followed Charlotte as her cousin crossed the yard toward their buggy. Suddenly, Charlotte stopped and Rachel nearly bumped into her.

"Noah, would you like any of these cookies?" Charlotte asked. "Annie Zook made them."

Rachel didn't hear his response. She was trying desperately to move away, to give them time to visit alone. But as she hurried to turn, she tripped, and it was Noah who was suddenly there to steady her, his hand warm through her long dress sleeve.

Blushing, Rachel was saved from having a conversation with him when Aunt Mae appeared to urge them into the buggy. She could feel Noah's gaze as she climbed inside. She didn't glance back, but kept her eyes trained ahead.

Rachel hated that he had this strange effect on her. She had to avoid him as best she could without things appearing odd to anyone. Earlier in the day, several of the neighbor women had wondered aloud why Noah and Charlotte had not begun to court openly yet, but even if they were not official sweethearts, Rachel would not interfere. "It's only a matter of time," Miriam Zook had assured a small group of women when neither Katie nor Aunt Mae was present.

Since then, every time Rachel was affected by Noah's presence, she felt a sense of betrayal toward her cousin, guilty about the way Noah made her feel. She knew what it felt like to be betrayed…and it was the worst thing she'd ever experienced.

Chapter Five

The day was warm, with a stiff breeze that tore at the garments Rachel and Charlotte were hanging to dry. Rachel secured cousin John's overalls on the clothesline. Satisfied that the wooden clothespins would hold, she bent and lifted a wet mint-green shirt, enjoying the warmth of the sun on her face as she pinned it into place next to the overalls. The linen scent of detergent mingled with the aromas about the farm…the bright-red roses planted in the yard near the house…the smell of the family cow in a nearby pasture…the freshly tilled earth in the vegetable garden.

The wind tugged a dress from Charlotte's hands and sent it flying across the yard toward her cousin. "Rachel!" she cried. "Get it!"

Rachel laughed as she quickly caught the damp garment before it hit the ground. "I almost missed it."

"*Gut* catch," her cousin said with a grin. She looked carefree and happy in a pale blue dress, white apron, and white prayer *kapp*.

Rachel returned her grin as she hung the dress. "These clothes won't take long to dry in this weather."

"*Ja.* It's the perfect day for laundry," Charlotte agreed as she reached into the basket for her sister's black apron. "*Dat* and BJ are going to clean out the side room in the barn for this Sunday's singing," she continued, referring to her brother John, often called BJ, for Big John, when the family gathered. Little John was Sarah and Eli's son—Charlotte's nephew. "I think *Dat* is afraid if we stay in the house we'll keep him up at night with our songs and fun."

"It's a *gut* space," Rachel said. She grabbed a black prayer *kapp* and pinned it on the line. "How many will come?" The young people's singing was an event held the evening of each church Sunday, usually at the same farm or home as the church services that morning. It was a time for young men and women of the community to intermingle for song and fun. Rachel had always enjoyed singings in her Millersburg community in Ohio.

Charlotte looked thoughtful as she continued to hang clothes. "There will be four of us—you, Nancy, BJ and me…the four oldest Lapp boys. The Zooks and Mary Hershberger…"

Noah will be coming, Rachel thought, a little disturbed to realize that she was pleased.

"And then there will be some young people from the next church district…I'm not certain how many." Charlotte bent for a shirt and nearly collided with Rachel, whose thoughts had drifted. She laughed as she drew back quickly. "I don't know. Fifteen or twenty?"

It would be a large gathering. "We'll have a wonderful time," Rachel said.

Charlotte grinned. "*Ja.* Lots of *gut* food, fine singing and wonderful company."

The young women finished the chore and headed toward the house, their spirits high and their appearance disheveled from the wind that had loosed fine strands of hair from their pins.

"We've finished, Aunt Mae," Rachel said as she entered the house. She reached up to attempt to fix her hair and then gave up, unsuccessful. "What else can I do to help?"

"You've done enough, Rachel. Why don't you head toward the *schuul* to see how the construction is coming on the teacher's cottage?"

"*Ja,*" Charlotte urged her. "You said you'd enjoy watching the work take place."

Rachel nodded. "But surely there is more you'd like me to do first."

"*Nay,*" Aunt Mae said. "Horseshoe Joe came by for Uncle Amos early this morning. They went over to Abram Peachy's house. I told Amos that we'd come for him before supper.

"Your new *haus* is not far, and it's a nice day for a walk. Just head up the lane and turn right. Be careful," she warned, "of speeding cars along the narrow road." She rolled her eyes. "Some of these Englishers drive like…"

Rachel nodded, pleased with the idea of visiting the cottage. "I will." She knew her hair must look a sight. Should she head upstairs to put herself to rights first? The breeze would only pull her hair free…unless she put in extra pins.

She debated whether to fix her hair when Aunt Mae approached. "You can take these muffins for the workers. I'm sure they would enjoy something to eat about now."

Charlotte came up from behind her mother and handed Rachel cups and a water jug. "The Lapp men will be thirsty as well."

"Go along now, Rachel." Aunt Mae didn't see anything wrong with the way she looked, Rachel realized, so it must be all right for her to go just as she was. Besides it was wrong to worry about one's looks. Vanity was a sin that she wouldn't give in to.

With a brown paper bag filled with sweet muffins and cups in one hand and the jug of water in the other, Rachel started down the dirt lane that led through the King property toward the main road.

The sun felt wonderful, and Rachel tilted up her face to enjoy its warmth. A fly buzzed about her ear and, laughing, she swatted it away. The warm breeze held the scent of fresh-tilled earth and the honeysuckle that grew along one side of the lane. Rachel felt a deep sense of peace and contentment as she walked.

Would she see Noah at the house? Her heart gave a little thump. She hadn't seen him since Sunday. While she fought hard to get him out of her mind, she couldn't forget his face, his endearing smile and the many kindnesses he had shown her.

She reached the end of the dirt lane and waited at the edge of the paved road until a car sped past before she ventured to cross the street. She turned right and continued along the roadway, facing traffic. She smiled as she caught a glimpse of the schoolhouse and hurried on. With her heart buoyed by lightness, she approached a window and peered inside.

She grinned. She loved the rows of desks and the larger one in the front of the room. The schoolhouse was empty. Would it be unlocked?

She tried the door and realized that it was necessary to lock it when no one was about. *Such a shame.* She would have liked to wander around inside again.

Soon, she thought. Soon she would be standing before her class of eager students.

Rachel rounded the building and headed along the dirt drive toward the teacher's cottage. The day was quiet. The only sounds she could hear were an occasional insect or a passing car on the main road and the breeze stirring the nearby trees and her dress hem and apron. Perhaps the Lapps couldn't find time to work on the house today, she mused, disappointed.

Unlike the school, the cottage door stood partially open. With a frown, she hesitated only a few seconds before pushing the door in and entering.

"Samuel? Jedidiah? Noah?" she called out. "Is anyone here?"

"In the back of the *haus,* Rachel!" Noah appeared within seconds. "You've come to see the construction," he said, sounding pleased.

Her senses humming at the sight of him, Rachel nodded. "I brought muffins and a jug of water."

His eyes were warm as he smiled. "I am hungry and could use a drink." He waved her to follow him. "Come and see what we've done."

Eagerly Rachel followed Noah toward the rear of the house, her neck tingling as she studied his back. He wore a royal-blue shirt under his denim overalls. She watched as he lifted his wide-brimmed straw hat, ran his fingers through his silky, sandy-brown hair before settling the hat back onto his head. There was a fine sheen of moisture across his nape. She tried not to look at his neck, glancing instead at the house as they walked through.

"Is Samuel here?" she asked.

"Nay," Noah said without turning. "I am the only one working." Suddenly, he spun to smile at her, and

the impact of his twinkling, warm brown eyes made her head spin and her heart leap within her chest. "I told you that the house would be done in a month. It may take a little longer."

He nodded toward the kitchen area. A brick hearth had been built since her last visit. The walls had been insulated and the drywall hung. The room was large, bright and inviting. She could picture those walls white-washed and a table with chairs in the center of the room.

"A fine *kiche*," she said. She imagined the kitchen as it would one day be, filled with the smells of good food cooking and company gathered around the table.

"My *grossdaddi* is making the kitchen cabinets," Noah told her, helping to paint a better picture for her. "I think you will like them. He does *gut* work."

Both the school and the house seemed to solely be the work of the Lapp men, and she mentioned this to Noah.

"We've had help from all," he said. "We had a house-raising for the initial framework. But this land once belonged to *mein grosselders* and there was time before the house needed to be completed. With the spring planting, we worked when we were able…to make sure everything was right for the teacher in our community." His voice softened. "*You. Grossdaddi* is a kind man."

Like *grossdaddi,* like *kinskind,* she thought. The man's grandson Noah, too, was kind. "Noah, everything is very nice. I know I will be happy here."

Her words trailed off as their gazes met and something warm passed between them. Flushing, Rachel glanced away.

"I am glad, Rachel." Noah studied the young woman before him, noticing how appealing she looked with soft tendrils of hair about her face and neck. She wore a lavender dress with a white cape that tucked into the waistband of her white apron. A matching white prayer *kapp* covered her shining dark hair. She had the prettiest eyes…large and glistening. He could feel himself drowning in her gaze, felt the pull of her nearness. He drew a sharp breath and looked quickly away. He hadn't expected to see her today, and the pleasure he felt seeing her, hearing her voice, was beyond anything he'd ever experienced.

There was a brief but potent moment of silence. Noah felt impelled to break it. "Would you like to see more of the construction?"

She seemed relieved as she nodded. "You have done a lot in one week's time."

"There is still much to do, but we will be finished before school starts."

"May I look around?" Rachel asked.

"Ja," Noah said with a grin. "Come. I'll show you more and explain what we will be doing next."

Rachel enjoyed the tour of the house with Noah as her guide. He showed her where the bedroom would be, the parlor or front room and the pantry, where she would be able to stock her canned and baked goods.

Every step of the way, Noah was conscious of Rachel beside him. He could hear every tiny exhalation of her breath, detect the clean scent of her skin. He could feel the warmth that radiated from her to him. She smelled like sunshine and rose-petal soap.

"You will have all that you need to be comfortable," he said.

She followed him as he stepped outside the house.

"Preacher Stoltzfus and his family are donating the stove and freezer," he said, "and the Zooks have given money toward a new gas refrigerator." Before Rachel could comment, Noah continued. "We will put a clothesline here." He gestured to a grassy area in full sun. "I will make the wooden T-bars for the line myself—"

"Rachel!" Samuel, Noah's father, came up the dirt driveway. He carried a handsaw and a carpenter's tool belt. "You like the house," he said knowingly.

Rachel glanced over in surprise that he could read her thoughts. "It is wonderful."

Samuel looked pleased. "Abram Peachy and your uncle Amos will be helping us to finish the floors."

"Rachel brought muffins and water, *Dat*."

"Aunt Mae's muffins," Rachel said. She liked Noah's *dat*. He was a gentle man with a ready smile. *Noah is like him,* she thought, but then was embarrassed by her own thoughts.

"Tell Mae we appreciate the muffins."

Rachel nodded. "May I see inside the *schuulhaus* again?" she asked.

"Ja." Samuel grinned. "You will enjoy teaching?"

Rachel grinned back as she inclined her head. "I am glad I was asked to come. Everyone in Happiness has been kind to me."

"We are glad that you came to us," Samuel replied. "You will be good for our children. Come and I'll open the school for you."

"You are easy to be kind to," Noah said softly as they trailed behind Samuel.

Surprised by the intensity of his tone, Rachel flashed him a look and was stunned by his expression. It was almost as if he liked her, felt the same little thrill that she experienced whenever they were together. But that couldn't be... It was Charlotte who had stolen his heart and affections.

Samuel unlocked the schoolhouse door and then

handed Rachel the key. "For you. So you…can come and visit whenever you wish. I'm sure there is much to be done before a new session of school starts."

Rachel was touched by Samuel's thoughtfulness. She saw Noah in his father's face. *Is this what Noah will look like in the years to come? Cousin Charlotte is lucky to have a good and kind man,* she thought.

Samuel and Noah accompanied Rachel inside the schoolhouse and reported on the progress made since her last visit.

"You now have writing paper and pencils," Samuel said.

"We have installed a pencil sharpener," Noah added.

Eyeing the metal crank sharpener, Rachel beamed. "I'm eager to begin."

"The first day of class will be here in no time," Samuel said.

Rachel noted that the *schuul* room still smelled like newly varnished wood but she could detect additional scents…of paper and chalk, pencil shavings—someone must have tried out the pencil sharper, she thought— along with the roses that someone had left in a vase on the teacher's desk. The combined scents reminded her of her own *schuul* days and the joy she'd gained from learning English and math and other important lessons for life.

Shortly afterward, they returned outside.

"We'll be putting in two swing sets for your students to use at recess." Samuel showed her where they planned to construct the swings.

"Two! How wonderful," Rachel said. The nearest *schuul* to her parent's home had an old swing set in the yard, and she had often watched how much the children enjoyed it. With the number of students she expected in her classroom, she realized that they would need more than one set.

"There will be a bench for you there," Noah said. "I should be done with it soon."

Rachel felt her throat tighten with emotion. The Lord had brought her to this new home, and now she was beginning to see that He had decided that she and Abraham were not meant to be together. Some of her burden of pain began to ease. There were feelings, though, that would take longer to resolve, but with the Lord's help, she would settle them.

"I'd best get back to work." Samuel's sincere gaze warmed her. "You come here whenever you'd like." He nodded at his son. "You will help with the floors?"

"Ja."

Samuel smiled. *"Gut."*

"I will see you Sunday, Rachel," Samuel said.

"Ja, Samuel," Rachel said. "Thank you for building me such a *gut* house. I am grateful for your hard work."

"Sunday service is at your aunt's," Noah said quietly after his father had gone back inside the cottage.

"We have been baking cakes and pies." She felt tingling along her spine whenever she was in Noah's presence.

Noah's eyes lit up. "What flavor did you bake?"

"Strawberry," she said, thrilled by his reaction. "And chocolate."

He grinned. "I will enjoy having more of your pies."

Her reaction to his grin made her glance away. She should have come with her cousin. Noah was Charlotte's friend; she should not be feeling anything but friendship whenever she was with him. The closest thing she'd ever felt to this was when she and Abraham Beiler first started to walk out together. Only this feeling with Noah seemed more…intense.

Guilt made her stomach churn. She sent up a silent prayer that God would help her to control her feelings, to remember that she and Noah were meant only to be friends. The sound of a buggy's wheels and the clip-clop of horses' hooves on macadam made Rachel glance to the road, where she caught sight of Charlotte behind the reins of the Kings' gray family buggy.

"Rachel!" she cried. "I'm headed over to Abram Peachy's for *Dat.* Care to go with me?"

Noah stepped out and waved to her. "Charlotte," he greeted with a grin.

"How's the construction coming, Noah?" she asked, grinning back.

"Comin' along." He gestured toward the cottage. "Do ya have time to take a look?"

"Nay." She appeared disappointed. "But I'll stop by to see it the next time Rachel wants a look."

Rachel smiled at Noah before hurrying toward the King buggy. "I enjoyed the tour, Noah. The teacher's house is looking fine."

"A few more weeks, and it will be done." He nodded toward the school. "We'll have the swing sets finished as well."

"A swing set," Charlotte said, looking pleased. "The children will enjoy that."

"Ja," Rachel said as she climbed into the buggy to sit beside her cousin. She could envision the *kinner* at play.

"We will see ya at Sunday church service," Charlotte said to Noah.

He nodded, and with a last quick look in Noah's direction, Rachel settled in to enjoy the ride with her cousin and remind herself that Noah had just been nice to the new schoolteacher when he took her on a tour of the house and school. It was Charlotte who was his friend, Charlotte who had his interest.

"I promised to watch Abram's younger children whenever he and *Dat* head over to work on your new floors."

"That is thoughtful of him to help," Rachel said.

Charlotte nodded. "Abram Peachy is a fine man."

Rachel looked at her, surprised by her cousin's tone, but nothing about Charlotte's expression gave away her thoughts.

"Noah showed you the progress?" Charlotte said.

"*Ja,* as he said, the house is coming along." Rachel sat back to enjoy the weather and the day. "Did you see the kitchen fireplace? *Gut* craftsmanship. I will enjoy using that."

"And you will have a gas stove as well."

"I learned to cook on a fireplace," Rachel said. "I will use both." She leaned closer to the side window to watch two Amish children at play. It jogged her memory. "Noah said that there will be two swing sets in the school yard."

"Two?" Charlotte said as she steered the buggy onto a dirt road that led to a farmhouse surrounded by newly planted fields. "You will need both sets for thirty-one students."

Rachel beamed. "I am eager to see them."

The buggy's wheels kicked up a small cloud of dust as Charlotte steered the vehicle into Abram Peachy's barnyard. Driving the buggy close to the house, she pulled back on the reins and the old family mare settled to a stop.

Abram immediately came out of the house as if he'd

been watching and waiting for them. His gaze went first to Charlotte.

"Charlotte." Abram nodded shyly. "Rachel."

"Abram," Charlotte greeted. "*Dat* ready to come home?"

"*Nay.* In fact, he thought this afternoon would be a *gut* time to head over to the *schuul* yard to build the swing sets. Can you stay and watch Ruthie and Jacob? Nathaniel and Jonas are at the Masts', helping William. Mary Elizabeth will be leaving for town soon with Alta and Sally Hershberger. Rachel, I didn't know you'd be coming—do you mind if Charlotte stays? We could give you ride back home if you'd rather not."

"I don't mind staying," Rachel said with a smile. "I am happy that you are helping with the schoolyard swings." She saw the man redden slightly. There was kindness in the man's features, a trait her cousin seemed to appreciate, if Rachel could read Charlotte's expression accurately. She understood why Abram had been made deacon in the church.

Charlotte had remained quiet at first. She got out of the buggy and rounded to where Abram stood waiting.

"How is Ruthie today?" Charlotte asked.

Abram's smile told of his affection for his youngest. "She is eager for you to stay with her."

"I brought a pie and a few other things for the children's lunch."

"I'd appreciate it if you'd save me a piece of the pie," Abram said.

"*Nay,*" Charlotte replied and Rachel saw the man's face fall. Her cousin must have noted his expression, too, for she grinned and reached into the buggy to show that she had brought another dessert. "For you, I brought some peach cobbler."

Abram's eyes crinkled with delight. "Peach cobbler. You made it?"

"Ja," Charlotte said. "From peaches we canned last summer. They are the sweetest we've ever tasted. I don't know what we'll do if this year's fruit isn't as tasty."

He beamed at her. *"Danki."*

Abram's three youngest came out of the house— Ruth, Jacob and Mary Elizabeth. Spying Charlotte, little Ruth ran to throw her arms about the young woman's waist.

"Charlotte!" The little girl wore no bonnet, and her hair was coming loose from its back roll. "Mary Elizabeth tried to do my hair, but it keeps falling." She looked up at Rachel's cousin with big blue eyes. "Will you fix it for me?"

"Ja, Ruthie. Go back inside, and we will join you." Charlotte placed a hand on the girl's shoulder. "You remember Rachel?" Ruthie nodded. "No need to worry, Abram. All will be well here. I'm going to start by repinning Ruth's hair."

Abram nodded, appearing grateful. *"Danki,* Charlotte—Rachel."

"We are here to help, Abram," Rachel said. "Go assured that we shall take *gut* care of your children."

"I know you will," he told Rachel.

Amos King, Rachel's uncle, came out of the barn and approached. "You came with Charlotte."

"Ja, Uncle Amos." She had climbed out of the buggy, and now she waited before securing the horse to the hitching post. "Will you take the family buggy?"

"We'll take my wagon," Abram said.

"We'll stop by the house to tell Mae that you'll be staying at Abram's," Amos said as he climbed into

Abram's wagon and took his seat beside the kind widower.

Rachel watched as the men waved and Abram steered his mare Mattie in the direction of the school yard. "Abram, we will have supper ready when you get back!" she called out.

Abram acknowledged her comment with a wave and a grin. Rachel turned and headed into the house to help her cousin watch the Peachy children and clean the house.

Within moments, Alta Hershberger came in her open market wagon for Mary Elizabeth, and Charlotte and Rachel were left to mind the two youngest Peachy *kinner* and enjoy the afternoon.

On Friday of church-Sunday weekend, Rachel heard the wheels of the bench wagon as it pulled into her uncle's barnyard. From the house, she watched as Noah and two of his brothers jumped off the back of the wagon and began to unload. The wooden benches were long and backless and used for every Sunday church service. The day before, Uncle Amos, with Sarah's husband, Eli, their son David and cousin John had cleared the great room of furniture to make room for the bench seats.

Rachel, Charlotte and Nancy had spent the latter part of the week cooking, baking and preparing for Sunday services and the shared meal afterward.

Soon, Sunday morning arrived and at eight o'clock came members of their church district. Noah climbed down from his family wagon and headed straight for Rachel, his gaze focused only on her. Rachel felt a rush of joy, which she quickly checked as she glanced toward her cousin and others around to see if anyone had noticed. No one seemed to note anything untoward in Noah's behavior. Rachel closed her eyes with relief, and when she opened them again, Noah stood directly before her. He held his hand outstretched toward her with something on his palm. "Here is your key."

Rachel blinked. "To the house?"

"Ja." Noah grinned at her reaction, enjoying her surprise mixed with stunned pleasure.

"It cannot be finished."

"Nay," he agreed. "But we would like you to come and go as you please to see the progress."

She was touched by his—and no doubt his father's—thoughtfulness. She smiled her thanks as she accepted the key. She stared down at the brass object, feeling the weight of it in her hand, knowing that with it came the responsibility of educating their Amish community's children.

"Noah." Charlotte approached and saw what Rachel was holding. "How wonderful!" If she sensed attraction of any kind between her cousin and Noah, she didn't show it. She seemed genuinely glad for Rachel. "Will you take us through the house tomorrow?"

Noah nodded.

"Noah! Charlotte!" Aunt Mae called.

It was time for Sunday services. Obediently they filed into the King house and took their seats on the benches set out for them. The men were on one side, the women on the other. The benches filled three sides of the room, with the fourth side for the preacher who would conduct the service.

Noah's gaze met Rachel's from across the room. Feeling her face heat, she quickly glanced downward before focusing on the minister. She could feel the intensity of Noah's attention, but she refused to glance his way, focusing instead on the word of God. The congregation began to sing from the *Ausbund,* the book of hymns.

Rachel thought she heard Noah's voice above the rest, but realized that with her continued thoughts of him, she had probably just imagined it.

As they moved from the *Loblied,* the second hymn always sung at every church service as well as at weddings and other sacred events, Rachel listened intently as Preacher Levi Stoltzfus spoke about God's word. He talked with great emotion, and Rachel could feel the depth of his passion for the *Ordnung,* his deep belief in the Amish faith. She felt the love of God and the warmth of His people as she sat in church in her aunt's home.

Soon, they were singing a third hymn from the *Ausbund.* Rachel glanced in Noah's direction, but then hurriedly looked away when she realized that Noah had continued to study her throughout the entire Sunday service.

Chapter Six

After the congregation sang the last hymn, Preacher Levi closed the service, and the church members dispersed for food and fellowship. The house instantly became a hive of noise and activity. The worship service had taken a little over three hours, and the children who had been good and obedient during church were ready to run about and burn off energy.

With purpose evident in her steps, Aunt Mae went straight to the kitchen, followed by her daughters and niece. The young men of their church district worked to move benches and set up tables in preparation to dine. The older men went outside to load any unused benches into the cart.

"Rachel," Aunt Mae said, appearing every inch the one in charge, "will you get the potato salad and coleslaw out of the refrigerator? Charlotte, see if any of the tables are ready and work with Nancy to get out the plates and utensils."

"Yes, *Mam*." Charlotte grinned at Rachel as they passed each other on the way to do Mae's bidding.

Rachel smiled as she heard her aunt address her eldest, married daughter. "Sarah, please check on the children and make sure they don't get into the desserts before dinner."

Conscious of the way Noah had watched her during Sunday service, Rachel headed toward the back room, where the gas-powered refrigerator and chest freezer were situated.

She opened the refrigerator. The appliance was full. The women of their church district had brought enough to feed the entire community. Rachel bent inside, searching first for the potato salad. She found the large bowl on the back of a shelf. Rachel rearranged and lifted several other food items so that she could reach the glass bowl of Aunt Mae's potato salad.

Rachel had trouble balancing what she held in her arms as she shifted another platter on the shelf to better reach the coleslaw.

"Here, let me take that," a familiar voice said.

Rachel gasped and nearly hit her head on the inside of the refrigerator. "What are you doing back here?"

"Offering to help you." Noah grinned at her as he relieved her of her armful.

Rachel stared at him, unable to respond or look away.

"Aren't ya going to find what you've come for?" he asked softly.

"Ja." Rachel quickly bent inside to retrieve the potato salad and coleslaw bowls. She stood carefully, only to find that he continued to study her. Blushing, she found a place to set down the bowls and then tried to gather the dishes Noah was holding.

He released them and Rachel set them back in the refrigerator. Noah was holding the potato salad and coleslaw when Rachel turned around.

"I can take them now," she murmured as she reached for the bowls while unwilling to meet his gaze.

"I'll carry them for you." Noah felt a spark of delight as he watched pink stain Rachel's cheeks.

"It's not necessary," she insisted. "Shouldn't ya be helping the men set up tables?"

"Nay." Noah studied her intently, making her face warm.

She arched her eyebrows as her eyes finally met his. "And why not?"

The corners of his lips tilted upward. "The tables are done, and the men are outside waiting to be called to supper." He held up his filled arms. "I prefer to help with the food." His voice softened. "To help *you.*" He grinned. "A much better pursuit than talking about today's weather or the growth of one's field crops. Besides, the potato salad may be Aunt Mae's, but the coleslaw my *mam* made."

Noah watched Rachel's changing expression as he spoke. Truth be known and admitted only to himself, he would rather spend the day in her company than do any other thing on the good Lord's earth.

He had enjoyed watching her during church service. He could tell she was as aware of him as he was of her. She met his gaze and then averted her glance. He saw her look about to see if anyone had noticed the silent interaction.

He liked Rachel Hostetler. He liked her a lot.

"What about Charlotte?" Rachel asked, interrupting his thoughts.

"What about Charlotte?" he echoed. Had he spoken his musings aloud? No, he realized. She would have looked mortified or pleased—whichever reaction she might have had if he had spoken how he felt about her.

"She will be looking for you."

"*Nay.* Charlotte has enough to keep her busy with Mae's directions."

At the mention of her aunt, Rachel stiffened. "Please," she said, "she asked me to bring the salads to the table. If I take too long, she will wonder—"

"Wonder what?" Noah teased.

"Noah!" Charlotte said as she entered the room. "Are you helping or hindering cousin Rachel?"

Rachel met her cousin's gaze with gratitude. "He's offering to help me, but I think he should be helping the men."

Charlotte laughed. "Rather than you?"

Rachel was surprised by Charlotte's reasoning. "He's like a younger brother. I think he enjoys teasing as much as helping."

"*Ja,* Rachel," her cousin answered. "You are most probably correct." And she didn't seem in the least concerned at finding her and Noah together in the back room.

Her cousin did not seem upset by Noah's attention to her. Were the women of the church district mistaken? Were Charlotte and Noah destined to be man and wife—or was it just wishful thinking on the part of the elders?

Noah had his way. He carried the potato salad and coleslaw to the main table where the men would be invited to dine. Rachel, in the meantime, had found Aunt Mae and pitched in to help carry in the meats and breads and vegetables.

"Rachel," her cousin Sarah said as she arranged cookies and muffins on a plate on the kitchen worktable, "you are enjoying our community?"

Rachel smiled, for she easily could admit the truth.

"*Ja.* I like Happiness and I'm eager to work with the students here."

"The teacher's cottage," she said, "it looks *gut?*"

Rachel nodded, noting again how much Sarah resembled Aunt Mae. "It will be done soon. The *schuulhaus* is ready, too. There will be swing sets for the *kinner.* The men have been working hard to ensure that all will be ready."

"Noah has been working there often," Sarah said.

Rachel's heart skipped a beat. "Noah and Samuel and Noah's brothers."

Her older cousin nodded. "You will have my John in your class."

Rachel smiled. Little John was Sarah's youngest son; David, her cousin's eldest, had finished the eighth grade over a year ago. "I will. John is a *gut* boy and smart. He does not think he needs to go, but I will show him differently. He will make a fine farmer, but he should know how to deal with the English."

Sarah agreed, but soon Eli approached to speak with his wife, taking her attention. Eli Schrock was a man of short stature, even shorter than his wife. His hair and chin-beard were dark, his build strong. Sarah made introductions between Rachel and Eli.

Dressed like the other Amish men of the community in his black Sunday best, Eli was polite and pleasant, his gaze recognizing her as a family member. He wore a black vest over a white shirt. His trousers matched his vest and wide-brimmed felt hat, which he wore low and that shaded his serious blue eyes. "'Tis *gut* to meet ya, cousin Rachel."

Rachel nodded and murmured an appropriate response. "And you, Eli."

Watching the interaction between husband and wife,

Rachel saw how suited Sarah and Eli seemed for each other. Their two youngest offspring, John and Rose Ann, were enjoying a game of tag nearby. Rachel caught the look of affection that glistened in Eli's eyes as he watched them at play.

This is what God intended, she thought. *A gut man loving and caring for his family.*

Would she ever find happiness with a family of her own? Rachel experienced a flash of pain as she recalled her courtship with Abraham Beiler and the plans they had made to have a family together. She no longer knew if a husband and children were in her future. In the Amish community, it was important for a woman to have a family, but it could be that the Lord had other plans for her.

Unbidden, an image of Noah's smiling face came to mind. Was it possible that the tiny spark she felt when she was in Noah's company was a sign sent by God to give her hope that she could someday have a husband? Not Noah, she assured herself quickly, but some other fine man? She sighed. She was afraid to care for a man. She'd felt betrayed by Abraham. Could she ever recover from his betrayal?

The men, including the church elders, came to the table to eat. The women served them, and then while the men enjoyed their food, the women and children ate in the kitchen. The King house wasn't as large as the Lapp residence, but all of the church members still fit nicely.

"It was a fine church service," Miriam Zook said as the women cleaned up afterward.

"Ja," Agnes Troyer said, "Preacher Levi is a blessing to us all."

"So is our deacon, Abram Peachy," Alta Hershberger commented as she wrapped up the leftover loaves of bread and set them on the table for others to take home afterward. "He is a man with a kind heart."

"She thinks every available man has a kind heart," Emma King whispered to Rachel. "Always looking for a husband for her Mary, poor thing. Mary can find a husband without her dear *mudder*'s help."

Rachel had to control a grin. Emma King was her cousins' *grossmudder*. She and *Grossdaddi* Harley had returned recently from a trip to North Carolina, where they'd been visiting relatives of Emma's. Charlotte's grandparents were outspoken and full of common sense. Meeting them for the first time, Rachel had liked them immediately.

Unaware of Emma's comments, Alta, Agnes and Miriam continued their conversation about Deacon Abram and his children.

Rachel couldn't help listening with interest. She looked at her cousin, who met her gaze with a barely perceptible smile curving her lips. Charlotte had seen Rachel listening to *Grossmudder* Emma.

"Do you think he will ever marry again?" Miriam put the lid on a bowl of pickled beets.

"Abram?" Alta arranged leftover muffins from different sources on one plate.

"Ja."

"'Twould be a shame if he didn't," Alta said. "Those five *kinner* of his need a *mudder,* and there are some girls in our community who need a husband."

The women finished cleaning up the table and moved outside to sit in chairs arranged in the front yard under a shade tree. The sun was warm and the sky was clear. Rachel thought they couldn't have asked for a nicer day.

Alta settled her attention on the two cousins who stood near their seats, waiting for Aunt Mae and some of the other women to come out into the yard. "Charlotte, Rachel, you would like to marry someday, *ja?*"

Rachel and Charlotte could only nod. It would have been a terrible thing to do any differently.

"Now, Alta and Miriam, don't you be planning any of my girls' weddings," Aunt Mae said as she joined the group. "There will be time enough when God wills it."

Rachel sat down, while Charlotte returned to the house. Katie Lapp joined the group, carrying baby Hannah. "May I hold her?" Rachel asked, loving the way the child had curled into her the last time she'd held her.

Katie smiled and handed over the sleepy little girl. "She feels comfortable with you," Noah's mother said. "You have a gift with children. You will be a wonderful teacher."

Rachel stood to settle the baby comfortably against her and then sat, ready to enjoy the afternoon. As the women chatted about the service, the meal and their children, she listened, content as she rubbed her hand over a dozing Hannah, who lay against her chest. She was conscious of the warmth of the baby against her and tears threatened. She closed her eyes so that no one would notice and willed the memory, the pain and fear, away.

A young boy's shout, followed by a woman's scolding, drew Rachel's attention. Opening her eyes, she couldn't help but laugh at what she saw. The second-eldest Peachy boy, eleven-year-old Nathaniel, had grabbed his sister's head-covering and was parading about the yard wearing Ruthie's Sunday black bonnet.

"Nate!" Charlotte King reprimanded, trying to look stern, but Rachel could see that her cousin worked hard to stifle her own amusement. "See how upset you've made your sister. Where is *your* hat?"

"Over there, Charlotte." He gazed up at her with wide eyes.

"Why don't you give Ruthie back her bonnet and put on your hat."

"*Ja,* Charlotte."

Charlotte nodded, approving his choice. As Nathaniel ran to do her bidding, she caught Rachel's gaze. Her eyes twinkled and Charlotte's lips broke into a grin. Rachel nodded and grinned back at her.

"Charlotte?" Ruthie Peachy drew Charlotte's attention. Rachel felt a little catch as the grateful little girl offered her hand to Rachel's cousin, and the two set off to enjoy a walk together.

Rachel closed her eyes again, but this time her thoughts were amused with visions of a little boy in his sister's bonnet.

"She'll make a *gut mudder,*" Alta Hershberger said, her eyes narrowing as she watched Charlotte and Ruthie walk away, hand in hand.

"*Ja,*" Aunt Mae agreed. "Charlotte, like my niece Rachel, has a way with children."

Hearing her name, Rachel opened her eyes. "Charlotte had a good teacher in her *mudder,*" she said lazily. Hannah stirred, and Rachel calmed her with a gentle hand on the back of her head. Katie Lapp had removed her daughter's *kapp,* as it was too warm for the child to be wearing it, especially when she had no need to wear one at her age.

"Alta, how is your *mudder?*" Katie Lapp asked.

The two women got into a conversation about Alta's ailing mother, who had problems with diabetes and arthritis, and Rachel listened, only partly hearing.

"Joshua!" Katie called a while later. "Will you find Amos or one of my sons for me?"

"Mam?" Noah appeared suddenly. "Were ya looking for one of us?"

"Ja, Noah. Joshua! No need to go looking for Amos." And Aunt Mae's youngest was only too happy to scamper away and play. "Once again, you are about when I need you," Katie said with a smile.

He had been near but out of sight for some time, watching Rachel as she held his baby sister. She'd looked relaxed and peaceful. *She'll make a* gut mudder. He could easily see her married and with children. As he'd watched, he'd realized suddenly that he wanted to be her husband. He wanted to be the father of her children. He saw her eyes pop open when she heard his voice, saw her stiffen and sit up straighter. Hannah started to cry but Rachel immediately soothed her.

"Noah?"

He quickly recovered himself. *"Mam?"*

"Would you tell your *vadder* that the cleanup is done here and we can go whenever he is ready?"

He focused his attention on his mother. *"Ja.* He is in the north field with Amos."

As he went to find his father, Noah couldn't dispel the mental image of Rachel holding Hannah, of the loving way she patted the baby's back and cradled the child's head. His feelings for Rachel reminded him of a conversation he'd overheard earlier between Miriam Zook and Alta Hershberger regarding his friendship with Charlotte. Many of the church district women believed that he and Charlotte would court, marry one day and then have a family. He might have entertained the idea a year or two ago…long before Rachel had arrived in Happiness.

But what of Charlotte? Did she expect them to wed? She was a dear friend; he certainly did not want to hurt her. Nothing had changed in their relationship to suggest that she had any intentions to have him for her husband.

He needed to speak with Charlotte and soon. He had to gauge her reaction and be honest with her. He owed her that.

She will make a great mudder *as well,* he thought as he recalled how she had scolded the youngest Peachy boy. He grinned. She had a strong sense of character and of right and wrong. He knew that Abram would have been distraught to see Nate teasing his little sister. Charlotte knew it as well. She had to be hard on the boy for Nathaniel's own good. And truth be told, Nate had obeyed without question. He hadn't seemed to mind at all.

Noah found his father in the north field, where he had seen him last. *"Dat!"*

The sun was bright as he approached, and he tugged down the brim of his black felt hat.

"Noah." His father waited patiently for him to join the men who had gathered to admire the field.

"Mam said that the cleanup is done and she is ready to leave when you are."

Samuel Lapp nodded and then turned to Amos. "You'll be getting ready for the singing."

Amos King agreed. "Jedidiah and the twins are helping BJ prepare the barn."

The singing held on the same Sunday as church service was a gathering of young people for the purpose of singing hymns from the *Ausbund* and for girls and boys to spend time together in an appropriate manner. A large table would be set up with seats prepared for the boys to sit on one side and the girls across from them. The singing would begin early evening and end about 10 p.m., but the young people would often stay longer to visit. The young men would take their sisters, but not the girls they were sweet on…although looks would definitely be exchanged between a young man and the girl he liked. Sometimes, the young man would ask to take his prospective girlfriend home. "You'll be attending the singing, Noah?" Amos King asked.

He had an immediate image of Rachel sitting at the table, her voice raised in song. "*Ja,* I will be there."

"Then I'd better see how the barn is coming," Amos said with a smile.

Samuel nodded. "And I'd better gather up my family and take them home."

Noah would attend the singing and gladly. He wanted the chance to spend time in Rachel's company. He couldn't take her home this night, as this was her home and she would not need a ride. Still, he would enjoy the opportunity to be near her.

Chapter Seven

That evening, Rachel stood outside the Kings' barn with her cousin Nancy, greeting the young people as they arrived for the singing. Amish teens from another church district would be joining them. There would be sixteen attendees in all, but it was Noah and his brothers who drew her attention as the Lapp buggy pulled into the yard and stopped. Rachel felt her insides begin to thrum as Jedidiah, Elijah, Jacob and finally Noah alighted and then approached. She tried to look away, but she couldn't keep her eyes off Noah.

"You have brought your singing voices?" Nancy teased with a smile.

"Ja," Elijah Lapp said shyly.

"What singing voices?" Jacob eyed the cousins with a grin. "Who said anything about singing voices? I thought we were here to—"

"Jacob!" Jedidiah scolded. "Mind what you say to Nancy and Rachel."

Unembarrassed by the exchange, Rachel grinned at Jacob and then Jedidiah before she greeted Elijah. Lastly, she felt a little thrill as she spoke with Noah.

"Did you bring your appetite?" she teased Noah. "There are chocolate brownies and fudge candy."

Noah grinned. "*Ja,* I'm always hungry for chocolate."

Several other buggies pulled into the yard, drawing their attention. Rachel remained conscious of Noah beside her as Annie Zook, her brother Josiah, her sister Barbara and Mary Hershberger got out of a carriage and approached.

"Annie," Jedidiah greeted, "I heard you have a new dog. How is she doing?"

Annie regarded him with bright eyes as she nodded. "Millie is doing fine. She follows me all about the yard and house." She lowered her voice. "*Dat* lets me keep her inside."

The Miller sisters, Rebekka and Mary Anne, and their brother Reuben joined the gathering, and Nancy introduced them. Rachel stood and greeted the Millers and then each person she met: the Troyer brothers—Ron and Wayne, along with the Mast twins—Mark and Martha. She tried to remember their names, but her thoughts were filled with Noah, who had chosen to stand next to her.

"The Mast twins love M&M candy." Noah leaned close to whisper in her ear, and Rachel could detect his lemon-scented shaving soap. "Martha and Mark—M and M. Remember that and you'll know their names. They've probably brought some of the candy with them."

She chuckled. "Any other helpful hints?" she asked him.

Noah looked thoughtful. "RW for the Troyer brothers? Ronald and Wayne."

"RW? How am I to remember that?" Rachel stuck a hand in her apron pocket.

He shrugged but looked amused. "It was the only thing that came to mind."

The young people stood outside talking and teasing one another. The younger Lapp brothers, Elijah and Jacob, moved away from the group to speak privately. Rachel saw Elijah nudge Jacob as he gestured toward someone—Nancy, she thought—in the gathering of young women. Jacob scowled as he listened to his brother before he and Elijah headed back toward the barn. They stopped to let the girls go first, and then crowded each other in the doorway as Elijah tried to beat his brother inside, probably to find a seat at the table nearest to the particular girl he had his eyes on.

Noah waited outside when Rachel hesitated about entering the barn. "Would you like to go in?" he asked.

She nodded. *"Ja."* She was overly aware of the fact that they were the only ones in the group remaining outside. She felt a fluttering in her stomach. Noah looked wonderful in his white shirt and black vest. She glanced away from his intense regard, her gaze dropping to his black shoes, traveling up his black trousers to stare at his neck.

"A *gut* night for a singing," he said softly.

"Ja." Was that all she could think of to say? She could sense his amusement, which bothered her, so she pretended to be indifferent. "We should go inside."

Charlotte came out of the King house and waved as she crossed the yard. Spying her, Noah immediately excused himself. "I need to speak with Charlotte," he told Rachel. "Go ahead inside and we'll join you in a few minutes." He hurried from Rachel's side to meet Charlotte halfway across the yard.

Rachel felt her heart grow heavy to realize that he

hadn't even waited for her answer. Unable to watch the two deep in conversation, she turned and slowly entered the barn.

Noah hurried toward Charlotte. "May I talk with you?" This was the first opportunity he'd had to discuss privately the community's expectation of their courtship and marriage.

Charlotte frowned. "Is something wrong?"

Waving her to follow, he moved away from the barn so that their conversation couldn't be overheard. "We have been friends a long time, *ja?*"

"*Ja,* Noah. Since we were children."

"The community expects us to marry." He pushed back his hat and locked eyes with her.

She scowled. "Noah, you're not going to ask to court me, are ya?"

He waited a heartbeat to search for the right answer. "Have you been waiting for me to ask you?" This was Charlotte, his closest friend for many years. He didn't want to offend her.

"*Nay.*" She shook her head, her expression concerned as she gazed up at him. "Noah, may I tell you what is in my heart?"

"*Ja,* you can tell me anything." He stood leisurely with his hands in his pockets, waiting for her to respond, but he felt anything but calm.

"I care for another. At one time, I thought we might one day court and wed, but not now—"

Relieved, Noah grinned. "I too care for another," he confessed. He glanced toward the barn, at where Rachel had been standing earlier.

"My cousin Rachel."

He was surprised by her perception. "*Ja.*"

"Gut." She glanced briefly toward the barn, as if she was eager to join the others.

"You don't mind?" he asked, wondering if it was true. Was she glad that he liked Rachel?

She regarded him with twinkling blue eyes. *"Nay.* How can I mind when my heart wants Abram?"

Noah chuckled, happy with her revelation. "Abram Peachy." He raised his eyebrows. "And his five children. The little ones do love you. Has Abram shown an interest?"

"Not yet."

"Maybe I can help you—" He grew thoughtful. "What if I arrange it so that you get to spend time in Abram's company?"

She nodded, pleased. "And I tell Rachel about all your good qualities. I've seen the way she looks at you. She may like you but is too shy to show it."

He shrugged. "She doesn't seem shy to me."

"She doesn't know you as well as I do," Charlotte said as the two headed toward the barn. "But she will after she spends more time with you. What if we plan a trip into town? She'll feel comfortable with me there and it will give you a chance to talk with her. *Mam*'s been wanting me to shop for her. Are you busy tomorrow?"

"Tomorrow will work. Do you want to ask her or should I?"

"Let's see who has the first opportunity. If you get a chance first, you ask her. If the opportunity comes my way, then I will."

"All right. Let's hurry. I'd like to sit across from Rachel if the seat isn't already taken."

"Noah?" Charlotte said, and he halted, faced her. "Be yourself...and you'll win her heart."

He grinned at her as they continued toward the barn. "I can say the same about you and Abram. Abram is a shy man. He will open up more if he is comfortable. You've done a wonderful job with his children. They already love you. I think that Abram may care for you, but he is not yet ready to admit it to himself…or you. Let me think about it, and I'll see what I can do to help you to spend more time with him, and *not* cleaning his house or watching his children. Something more enjoyable for the two of you."

Jedidiah Lapp led the singing, his strong voice clear and vibrant. His brothers Jacob and Elijah and Mary Hershberger quickly joined in, and the others followed, their voices raised in Jedidiah's choice of song. Noah took a seat next to his brother and across from Rachel.

Rachel met his gaze as Noah sat and smiled at her. She attempted to smile back, but she knew that she'd failed miserably. She had no reason to be upset. She knew that Charlotte and Noah were friends, and she shouldn't be surprised that Noah wanted to talk with her cousin alone. But it was hard to watch him walk away from her and go to Charlotte. She wasn't jealous or envious—it was a sin to be either one. She felt sad.

Jedidiah sat across from Annie Zook, and Annie gazed at him as she sang his choice of hymn from the *Ausbund*. After everyone finished the hymn, it was Annie's turn to choose. Each teen would get a chance to select a favorite hymn. In between songs, there would be refreshments and other little games to make the evening fun.

The evening passed quickly. Rachel relaxed and began to enjoy herself. She was no longer upset. It was hard to be upset when she remained the focus of Noah's gaze and smile as she sang along with the others.

Soon it was time for all to head home.

"May I walk you to the house?" Noah asked Rachel as he came up from behind her.

"It's just across the yard." Rachel searched for Charlotte, but her cousin had disappeared, perhaps in the company of Nancy as she headed home.

He tugged on the bottom of his black vest. "I'd like to walk you across the yard," he said.

Uncertain what to think, she could only nod. Truth was…she liked spending time with him.

A full moon lit the night, making it easy for them to see. "Nice evening for a walk," he commented conversationally. He seemed reluctant to move.

Rachel glanced at him and caught him staring at her. "*Ja.* There is a cool breeze." She quickly averted her gaze. "A *gut* time to leave the windows open."

There was a long moment of silence, or so it seemed to Rachel.

"Charlotte asked me to take her to town tomorrow," Noah said. He leaned a shoulder against the barn and crossed his legs. "Will you come?" His stance seemed waiting…expectant.

Suddenly nervous, Rachel fiddled with her *kapp* strings. "Charlotte didn't mention going into town."

A mosquito buzzed in her ear. Noah straightened, raised his fingers as if to swat the insect away. He quickly dropped his hand to his side, as if he'd thought better of it. "She asked before the singing this evening."

Was that what they were discussing earlier? Rachel wondered.

"Charlotte may not want me to go." She began to

walk toward the house, and Noah followed her lead. "Aunt Mae may have chores for me."

"Charlotte wants you to come." He stopped and caught her arm before quickly releasing it, but not before Rachel saw something flash in his eyes. He continued across the yard. "I'm sure she'll ask you."

Did she dare go into town with Charlotte and Noah? Rachel wondered. She shouldn't; she liked being near Noah too much. Still, if they both wanted her to come, why shouldn't she?

She paused and turned toward him. "Will Joshua be coming for ice cream?"

Noah grinned. "*Ja.* I'm sure he'll want some."

"It was delicious ice cream." Smiling, she walked on, and he fell into step beside her.

"Then you will come?" he asked, sounding hopeful, his soft voice close to her ear.

Rachel inhaled sharply and fought the temptation to lean into him. "If Charlotte asks me and Aunt Mae does not mind."

"Charlotte will be shopping for Aunt Mae."

Another mosquito buzzed in Rachel's ear, and she stopped to swat it away. Noah's hand was there first, brushing the insect from her *kapp.* Their fingers touched briefly and withdrew.

His nearness in the semidarkness had a strange effect on her. "I'm here," she announced unnecessarily as she climbed the porch steps. She turned, placed a hand on the railing. "It was nice of you to walk me across the yard." Her voice sounded shaky to her own ears.

"The pleasure was mine," he said huskily as he leaned in closer to her. He withdrew but seemed reluctant to leave.

Rachel thought she heard him sigh. "I will see you tomorrow morning, Rachel."

She nodded, silent, and then she opened the door, stepped inside, and quietly closed the door.

"Rachel!" Charlotte came out of the kitchen, holding up an oil lamp. "Would you like some cake?" The light cast shadows on her features, making her eyes shine.

Rachel grinned as she trailed behind her cousin into the kitchen. "Chocolate?"

"Ja." Charlotte waved her toward a chair.

Rachel sat down at the table and accepted the plate of chocolate cake that Charlotte handed her.

"Would you like to go to town tomorrow?" Charlotte sliced a second piece of cake and took the seat across from Rachel. "Noah is going to take us. *Mam* gave me a shopping list."

Rachel paused with her fork midway to her mouth. "You want me to come?"

Charlotte frowned. *"Ja.* Why wouldn't I? We'll have a nice day."

"It would be fun to go." Rachel ate a bite of cake. "I haven't been into town since I first came. Will Noah bring Samuel's market wagon?"

Charlotte nodded as she finished swallowing a spoonful of icing. "He is a *gut* driver. You won't have to worry," she assured her cousin as if she'd suddenly recalled what had happened in town with the runaway hired buggy.

"I know he is." Rachel got up and went to a cabinet. She opened a door and took out two drinking glasses.

"Noah is a *gut* man, isn't he?" Charlotte said.

Rachel filled the glasses with water and returned to hand her cousin a glass before she sat down again. "He has been kind to me. His family has done a lot for the school and the teacher's house."

"He will make a wonderful husband someday."

Rachel shot her a glance and found Charlotte grinning at her.

"Noah makes quality furniture." Charlotte spooned up a taste of cake.

"I like the desks he made for the *schuulhaus*." Rachel tugged off her *kapp* and set it on the chair next to her.

"He makes chairs and house furniture, too. And he can make cabinets. His *grossdaddi* taught him well."

Rachel felt a little pang. It was obvious that Charlotte was in love with Noah. Her cousin couldn't stop talking about him...how kind and good he was...his ability to make quality furniture...

Charlotte must be thinking about marrying Noah and perhaps soon....

The conversation about Noah dwindled, for which Rachel was grateful. She had known that Charlotte and Noah had a special relationship. She forgot that fact every time Noah did something nice for her.

They finished their cake in silence and then decided to head to bed. Charlotte picked up the oil lamp and led the way. The house was quiet. Their footsteps echoed on the wooden stairs as they climbed to the second floor. The air held the scent of burning lamp oil and the lingering aroma of their evening meal of cold fried chicken and sweet-and-sour chow-chow.

"Charlotte," Rachel whispered as they reached the top landing, "are you certain you want me to come tomorrow?"

"*Ja,* why wouldn't I be?" Charlotte answered. "The day wouldn't be the same without you."

"I will come, then." No matter how difficult it might

be to see Charlotte and Noah together, she would go and try to enjoy the day.

They slipped into the bedroom with barely a sound. The windows had been open and the room had the fresh smell of the day's sunshine mingling with the rich floral scents of the night from outside.

"Nancy?" Charlotte whispered.

Rachel leaned toward the bed. "I don't think she's here."

"Who?" Nancy entered the room with a pleased look on her face.

"Where have ya been?" her sister asked, studying Nancy from beneath lowered eyelids.

"Jacob and I were talking. He walked me home."

Charlotte grinned. "Jacob Lapp?"

Nancy scowled at her. *"Ja."* She dropped down on the end of her bed, which squeaked softly under protest.

"You had a nice time," Rachel said quietly.

"I did." Nancy removed her black prayer *kapp* and reached over to hang it on a wall peg. She began to remove her hairpins. "Jacob is nice. I like him, and I think he likes me."

Rachel wasn't surprised. From what she'd seen, Jacob was interested in someone, and Elijah probably had been teasing his brother about Nancy.

"All the Lapp men are nice," Charlotte said. "But if you like him, I hope he likes you the same way."

With the pins out of her hair, Nancy donned her nightgown. When Rachel and her sister had done the same, Nancy turned out the oil lamp while Charlotte and Rachel climbed into bed.

"It was a great night," Charlotte said.

Rachel could hear the rustling of the bedsheets as Charlotte and Nancy got comfortable. Thoughtful, she was silent for a long moment. "A great night but a long day. I'm suddenly tired."

"Me, too," Charlotte said softly.

"*Gut* night," Rachel murmured.

"*Gut* night," her cousins echoed sleepily.

The two weeks that followed passed by quickly with several days of rain. The trip to town with Noah had been canceled due to the wet weather. Since the rain cleared, everyone had been too busy to take the buggy to Miller's. Aunt Mae had garnered some of the supplies she'd needed from Katie Lapp. The rest could wait until there was time to visit Miller's Store.

Rachel had kept occupied helping her aunt with chores, and when she was done at the King residence, working with Charlotte at Abram Peachy's house. The next Sunday church service was to be held at Abram's. With no wife to ready the house for him, he was happy to see Charlotte, Nancy and Rachel arrive to clean and cook and keep an eye on the children while Abram went about his chores.

"Mary Elizabeth, would you like to make a cake with me?" Charlotte asked as she tied on a patched but clean work apron.

"*Ja,* that would wonderful," the little girl said, looking pleased.

"What about me?" little Ruthie piped up as she entered the kitchen.

Charlotte smiled. "I have something special for you to do as well. Have ya ever made pudding?"

Ruthie shook her head. "We ate pudding together."

"*Ja,* we did. What kind of pudding would you like to eat on Sunday? Chocolate?" She opened a cabinet and pulled out a large porcelain bowl.

Ruthie nodded vigorously. "And I can help?"

"You can help," Charlotte agreed. She tied her *kapp* strings to keep them from swinging too close to the stove while she cooked. She then reached to remove Ruthie's *kapp* and set it on the table, out of harm's way.

Nancy came out of a back room. "Charlotte, I think we need to clean out Abram's refrigerator. I'm not sure everything is safe to eat."

"He receives a lot of food from our friends and neighbors," Charlotte told her. "Probably more than he and the children can eat."

Nancy wrinkled her nose. "Some of it is not something a child would want to eat, and I'm sure Abram is too nice to turn someone's generous offering away."

Rachel checked through the cabinets for baking supplies. "We may have to go to Miller's Store for a few things. I don't see any vanilla or cocoa powder."

"*Mam* has extra," Charlotte said as she pulled a bowl out of a cabinet. She hunted through a drawer for some utensils. "Would one of you mind taking Abram's buggy back home for what we need?"

"I could go," Nancy said after a quick look at Rachel.

"I can drive the buggy," Rachel offered, but a knot of fear became lodged in her throat.

Chapter Eight

Rachel realized that she was right; Nancy didn't want to go after the baking supplies. *I can do it,* she told herself, *and I'll be fine.* She hadn't driven a buggy in over a year, but she would drive one today. "What else will we need?"

"I'll make a list," Charlotte said, searching through a drawer for paper and pencil. "While you're gone, we'll finish cleaning the bedrooms upstairs. Mary Elizabeth, Ruthie, would ya like to help us?"

"May we?" Mary Elizabeth asked just as Ruthie exclaimed, "*I* would!"

With list in hand, Rachel went outside and unhitched the horse. Telling herself to remain calm, she settled herself into the King family buggy and picked up the reins with shaking hands. She took several deep breaths, then, with a click of her tongue and a light flick of the leather straps, she guided the horse in the direction of her aunt and uncle's farm.

She was more than a little nervous at first. She hadn't driven since before the buggy accident that had hospitalized her for nearly two months, but soon the tension lifted and she started to feel at ease. It was a lovely warm June day, and she encountered little traffic on the roadway. She enjoyed the gentle roll of the carriage and the clip-clop sound of Mattie's hooves on the macadam.

A car came around a bend, startling her, and she held her breath and waited as the vehicle slowed as it passed.

How fast the Englishers go! They have little time to enjoy the simple things in their racing cars...the sights and sounds of early summer...the bright colors of rudbeckia or black-eyed Susans that grow profusely along the roadway and in folks' yards...the scent of clean, damp laundry drying on the clothesline.

As she drove along the road, she spied a familiar face—Thomas Schrock, a young boy in their Amish community. Thomas was riding his Amish scooter bike, a two-wheeled bicycle without pedals that was propelled with one's foot.

"Rachel!" Thomas greeted with a wave. The young towheaded child was Sarah and Eli's ten-year-old nephew, son of Eli's brother Matthew and sister-in-law Jane.

"Where are you riding today?" Rachel asked.

"Going to visit my cousin John."

"Tell your aunt Sarah that I will be by to see her soon."

"I will." With a push of one bare foot, Thomas was off, riding down the road toward Rachel's cousin Sarah's house.

As Rachel drove by the schoolhouse on her way to the King farm, she saw Noah and Jedidiah outside the teacher's cottage working to trim the bottoms off several wooden interior doors lined up on sawhorses. She waved as they looked up.

"Rachel!" Noah greeted, and Rachel could see his

surprise in finding her alone in the buggy. With saw in hand, he approached. "It's nice to see you out and about."

"Your house is almost finished," Jedidiah said with a smile as he joined Noah. "Would you like to come see?"

"I would," Rachel said, "but I have to pick up a few baking supplies and get back to Abram Peachy's."

Noah nodded. "This Sunday's church services are at Abram's."

"*Ja,* which is why Charlotte is waiting for me to bring her unsweetened cocoa powder and vanilla."

"Will you stop by later?" Noah asked.

"Tomorrow if not today," Rachel said.

"You'll be able to move in the week after next," Jedidiah informed her.

"I'll try to come after I'm finished at Abram's. I'd like to see the house. It's been some time since I've visited. Charlotte and Nancy will want to see it, too."

Noah pushed back his hat with his free hand. "*Mam* is making you window curtains."

They would be plain white window coverings, nothing fancy, as was the Amish way, but useful for privacy. "That is kind of Katie." The mare danced lightly, and Rachel calmed her.

"She wants to know when you'll stop by to visit."

"Tell her I'll be by as soon as I can. We've kept busy in Aunt Mae's vegetable garden. It's coming along nicely. We've been picking weeds brought on by last week's rain." She wanted to stay and chat, especially with Noah, but she had to go. "I will try to come back, but if I don't make it, I will see you on Sunday."

"Be mindful of the traffic on this road, Rachel Hostetler," Noah said softly.

"I will." Then she was off again with a light toss of

the leathers until the vehicle reached the dirt lane that ran to the King home. Swallowing the nervous lump in her throat, she gently tugged on the reins, guiding the horse toward the farmhouse. The gentle animal responded and Rachel found herself even enjoying her return to independence. But as her fears receded, thoughts of Noah lingered, and she tried to force them away.

There was no time for Rachel or either King cousin to see the teacher's cottage that day. The next afternoon the three young women decided to walk to the schoolyard and cottage.

"Jedidiah said I can move in the week after next," Rachel said as they walked.

"I don't think I like you leaving us," Nancy replied.

"I'll miss you, too, but I won't be far, and you can come visit, and even stay the night when you can."

That seemed to cheer Nancy. "Charlotte, was Abram happy with how the house looked?"

Charlotte had been the last one to leave the Peachy farm. Abram and the children had brought her home after she'd made their supper. "He seemed pleased. The girls enjoyed helping us."

"Ruthie likes chocolate pudding as much as vanilla," Rachel said with a smile.

Charlotte's gaze held a look of fondness for the child. "She had chocolate all around her mouth before she was finished helping."

"Mary Elizabeth had fudge icing around hers. She did well with cake baking. She'll be a good cook someday."

"As long as she has someone to teach her," Rachel said. "Such a shame that the children have no mother."

"I imagine he'll marry one day soon," Nancy commented.

A strange look passed over Charlotte's face. "What makes you think that?"

"It's what Alta Hershberger believes. She said Abram suffered the death of his wife hard, but he seems to be less burdened now. Once a man is less burdened, then it's only a matter of time before he can open his heart and home to a new wife."

"Alta Hershberger thinks a lot of things, but that doesn't make them true," Charlotte pointed out.

"Ja," Nancy agreed as she ran fingers over a honey-suckle bush as she walked.

"Has she decided who this new wife will be?" Charlotte stopped to pick a wildflower.

"Nay. She said Abram will decide when the time is right and he has made his choice."

Sunday came and went with church services at Abram's, but with the singing back at the Kings'. As he had the last time, Noah asked to walk Rachel to the house, and she accepted.

During the week that followed, members of the Amish community in Happiness came to furnish and finish the teacher's house. Rachel was pleased with the way the cottage looked and felt. It would be another week or so until her bed, table and chairs were finished.

Rachel joined the others in whitewashing the interior walls and sweeping the construction dust from the floors and counters.

"You should do well here," Aunt Mae said as she picked up a dust cloth.

"I will. I will miss living with you and Uncle Amos," Rachel said as she swept the kitchen floor. "I will miss my cousins."

"You're welcome to stay with us as long as you like

and to come back anytime. You may not want to move in until right before school starts. I don't know if I like the idea of you living here alone." Mae dusted the kitchen-cabinet doors.

"I'm not far from the farm," Rachel reminded her, "and the Lapps are just a few acres away."

"*Ja,* I suppose so." But Aunt Mae looked unconvinced. "You will let Charlotte or Nancy come and stay for a time?"

"Of course." Rachel paused in the act of sweeping an area near the base of a cabinet. "We're all family."

Aunt Mae's expression softened with a smile as the woman patted her niece's cheek. "You are a *gut* girl, Rachel Hostetler."

"It must be the blood we share," Rachel teased as she raised the broom again, and her aunt chuckled.

Charlotte appeared at the open back door. "Look what he's brought!" she cried excitedly before she hurried back outside.

Noah entered the kitchen carrying one end of a trestle table, his brother Jedidiah holding the other end. Behind him, brothers Elijah, Jacob and Daniel each brought in a matching chair.

"Thought you might like this now," Noah said as he set his end of the table down.

"I bet you didn't expect this today," Jedidiah added with a grin. He had the handsome Lapp male face, much like Samuel's and Noah's, but his hair was dark, and his chin had a slightly different set than Noah's. His eyes twinkled as he met her gaze before he turned to instruct his younger brothers on where to put the chairs. Elijah, Jacob and Daniel resembled both Katie and Samuel to varying degrees.

"There are more chairs in the wagon," Noah said,

and Rachel followed him outside with broom in hand. There were three more chairs, six in all.

"You made these?" Rachel asked Noah as she watched him hand down another chair to each brother.

"*Ja.* I would have had them done sooner, but I thought it important to finish the house first," he said.

Rachel nodded as she leaned against the broom handle. "You do fine work."

"The furniture is serviceable." He grabbed a step stool and carried it inside the house. He set it beside a cabinet. "For reaching the top shelf."

Smiling, she'd followed him back inside and set the broom against the wall. She was surprised to see Abram inside the house talking with Charlotte.

"Rachel, Abram brought you a rocking chair and a sewing box," Charlotte said, looking pleased.

"They are not new. The chair and box belonged to Elizabeth."

"I will need these, Abram." Elizabeth was Abram's late wife. Rachel realized how difficult it must have been for the deacon to lose someone so young. She caught a look between him and Charlotte, and her eyes widened.

She turned, her gaze settling on Noah, who was setting all the chairs in place around the table. Did it bother him to see Charlotte with Abram? Or was she seeing something that simply wasn't there?

She had thought that Charlotte's excitement had been in seeing Noah arrive with the furniture he'd made for the teacher's cottage. Had it been Abram who had drawn her attention and excitement and not Noah?

Studying Noah, she couldn't help but notice the difference between the two men. Noah was younger, with twinkling eyes and a ready smile. Abram was older, solid, and with kind eyes and a steady yet shy gaze.

Rachel watched her cousin. Charlotte stared at Abram, gazing at him particularly when he wasn't looking. Rachel frowned. What of Charlotte's relationship with Noah? Should she ask Charlotte? *The Lord will want me to mind my own business.*

The teacher's house was coming together. It wasn't ready for her to move in yet. She needed a bed, a stove and linens, as well as other essentials.

"You have all been kind," she told everyone who had come to help.

As they left, one by one, to return home for supper, Noah stopped before her and said, "It is easy to be kind to you, Rachel Hostetler."

His words gave her a lot to ponder on the way home.

That night Rachel thought of Noah as she lay, staring at the ceiling. The house was still. All was dark and quiet. Suddenly, she heard a double rumble of thunder.

"What was that?" Nancy said, sitting upright.

"I don't know," Charlotte replied. "I don't think it's a storm."

The rumble started again.

"I think it's the front door," Rachel whispered.

Charlotte sprang out of bed and into the hall. Mae stood on the landing with a flashlight.

"*Mam,* what is it?"

"Someone is at our door," Mae said. "Your *dat* went down to see."

"I hope no one is in trouble," Rachel said as she joined the other two at the top of the stairs.

Nancy padded out afterward. "What—"

"Shh!" her mother scolded. "I think it's Abram Peachy."

"Oh, no! I wonder what he wants."

"Amos." Abram stood at his friend's front door, looking distraught. "Jacob is missing."

Amos frowned as he stood back and gestured his friend inside. "How long?"

"I don't know. I thought he had gone to spend the night at your daughter Sarah's."

"Dat." Amos's son-in-law, Eli, followed Abram inside.

"Eli," Amos greeted. "You've not seen Jacob?"

"Nay. He was to spend the night with us, but the Zooks treated a group of youngsters to ice cream. I thought Jacob went, too, but then John came home alone. We've searched everywhere on Abram's farm, but not here."

"We should check here, then—and the Zooks'." Amos turned toward his wife, who was descending the stairs. "Jacob Peachy is missing."

"We will find him," Mae said firmly. She addressed her son-in-law. "Sarah and the children?"

"They are at home." Eli fidgeted as if he was eager to get on with the search. "They are upset and still looking, but she will stay home in case Jacob shows. Abram's other four are with them. We think it's best if they remain with Sarah while we look. We searched our property before we came here."

The cousins and Rachel, overhearing from upstairs, rushed to dress and join the others.

"We'll help," Charlotte said.

Rachel nodded. "I'll check Joshua's room," she offered.

Aunt Mae's eyes lit up. *"Ja,* do that."

Nancy said, "I'll go with Eli to the barnyard."

"I'll take Abram about the property. There are many

places a little boy might hide, and I know them," Charlotte said.

"I'll head over to the Lapps'." Amos hurried upstairs and returned in less than a minute, dressed. He grabbed his hat and settled it on his head. "Abram, Samuel and his sons will help us find him."

"Danki," Abram whispered to Charlotte as they headed out into the night, their path lit by the flashlight Abram carried.

"He'll be found alive and well soon, Abram." Charlotte caught and squeezed his hand before releasing it quickly. "Jacob is a *gut* boy, but he is easily distracted."

"Ja. The last time he disappeared, I found him in the barn, sleeping in the hayloft." He hesitated. "But not this time."

"Let's check the north field." She gestured in that direction. "There is an old lean-to there. Maybe he ran after an animal and took shelter there because he didn't know how to get home."

"I hope you are right, Charlotte." Abram trained the beam of the flashlight across the path before them. "I pray to the dear Lord that he isn't injured or hurt."

"I pray, too," Charlotte whispered as she stepped carefully over a rock.

Back at the house, Rachel waited with Aunt Mae. Jacob wasn't with Joshua, nor had Joshua seen his friend. Nancy had decided to search with Eli. Amos would return shortly with the Lapp men.

Rachel stood at the window, her heart filled with fear for a frightened little boy. He had been a joy to spend time with when she and Charlotte had watched Jacob and little Ruth earlier in the week. The boy had a lively sense of humor, and she looked forward to having him in her class. He was bright far beyond his young years.

She spied Amos's buggy and another that followed. "Uncle Amos and the Lapps are here." She went out onto the porch to meet them.

Amos climbed down from the buggy and approached. "Did ya find him?" he asked. He held his hat in his hands, and his hair looked as if he'd run his hands through it many times.

"*Nay.* Nancy and Eli are checking the barnyard and barn. Charlotte and Abram have gone looking over to the north field."

Amos looked worried. "We'll search all of our property before heading back over to the Lapps'. Samuel's boys are searching there.

"Samuel, you can come with me." He headed back to his buggy with Samuel following.

"I'll look with Rachel," someone said.

Rachel's breath caught as Noah stepped out of the darkness and onto the porch, his eyes glistening.

"Rachel," he greeted softly.

Chapter Nine

She stared at Noah in fascination. In straw hat, maroon shirt and denim trousers held up by suspenders, he looked wonderful…just as she'd thought of him only moments before.

"Aunt Mae?" she asked, her heart beating wildly. Would her aunt forbid her to join in the search…and with Noah?

"Go, girl. Find Jacob and bring him home." She had given three LED flashlights to the others. She rummaged in a drawer and discovered a fourth flashlight with an incandescent bulb.

Noah accepted the flashlight and waited for Rachel to join him. "Do ya have an idea where to look for him?"

Rachel frowned. "When I went into Joshua's room earlier to see if he knew where Jacob could have gone, my cousin said that Jacob was fascinated with a puppy he'd seen a couple of days ago. If the boy saw a stray or some kind of animal, it's possible he followed it."

Noah looked concerned as he gazed into the night. He clicked on the flashlight, which wasn't bright like an

LED light, but it allowed them to see. "It's so dark. If he is anything like my younger brothers, he'll be terrified."

"We have to find him," she said urgently.

"We will." Noah touched her shoulder, then as quickly pulled his hand away.

That light touch was enough to send her heart careening wildly. She inhaled sharply and tried to maintain her balance.

"Maybe we should check the schoolhouse and cottage," Noah suggested. "Jacob visited both the other day when Abram stopped by to find out when we planned to finish the floors. He seemed fascinated by the school… and the swing sets. He may have wandered down to play on the swings. When he realized that he had missed ice cream with the Zooks, he probably stayed to play. Later, after realizing how late it was, he may have found a way into one of the buildings to wait until morning before seeking help to get home."

"Shall we take the buggy?" Rachel asked, thinking it worth checking the school and cottage.

"*Nay.* It's not too far. Unless you're afraid of the dark?" he teased.

Most definitely not with him beside her, Rachel realized. "I'm not afraid. Let's go. We should tell someone where we are going."

"We'll probably pass Amos along the way. If not, we can get there and back before anyone worries." He looked concerned as they continued along the lane.

Was it wise? she wondered. He was probably right, but whether or not it was wise to walk alone with him was another thing.

The night held the sound of crickets and an occasional car on the main road ahead as she and Noah made their way toward the schoolyard. Rachel was quiet. She could hear the crunch of their feet on the dirt lane and the thunder of her own heartbeat.

Would Charlotte have chosen to search with Noah if she'd known he'd be arriving after she'd left with Abram?

Jacob, she thought. *If anything happens to him…*

"He'll be fine, Rachel," Noah said softly, as if reading her mind.

"I pray that it is so."

She could feel his gaze studying her and she turned to face him. "Do you think we can hurry?" She swallowed.

He nodded solemnly. "*Ja.* That is a *gut* idea."

They picked up their pace in unison, hurrying toward the road, running across to the other side. The buildings looked dark as they approached, which was no surprise, since the school and house weren't in use yet.

"Do ya have your key?" Noah asked as he dug a hand into a pocket of his trousers.

"Nay," Rachel said, upset. "I didn't think to bring it."

Noah grinned, his teeth a flash of white in the semidarkness, lit only by their flashlight. "I did." He held up a key, which glinted in the light.

She laughed. "You are a smart man, Noah Lapp."

He crinkled his nose and said simply, *"Ja,"* which only made her chuckle more.

The truth was Rachel felt nervous and scared, and at times, she laughed when all she wanted to do was to cry out or scream. Laughter was her way of coping. Did Noah think her awful for chuckling when the situation was worrisome?

They checked the schoolyard first, especially the area of the new swing sets, since Jacob had shown an interest in them. But there was no sign of him. Rachel looked closer and saw what could be scuffmarks in the dirt below one swing, but she couldn't be sure.

"Noah," she said, "would you bring the light closer?"

He quickly obliged, holding the light so they could carefully inspect the dirt. "It's possible he was here earlier…or someone else was. But it could have been any one of the *kinner* in our community."

"But no one knew that the swings were finished, except those families whose fathers constructed them. Jacob!" Rachel called.

Noah joined in with her. "Jacob!" they called together. They listened in silence for a response, but there was none.

"Do you think he may have somehow entered the school?" Rachel asked as she walked along the outer wall of the building.

Noah shook his head. "Not if it's locked." He had taken off his straw hat before he'd left the King farm, and she couldn't take her gaze off his glistening eyes, straight nose and clean-shaven jaw.

"May we check?" she started to say, but Noah was already rushing to unlock the schoolhouse door.

"Jacob?" Noah called. "Jacob Peachy? It's all right. You won't get in trouble, but your *dat* is worried about you. Come out and we'll take ya home. It's me, Noah, and I'm with Rachel Hostetler."

But the schoolroom remained silent.

Rachel felt tears fill her eyes. "It's so late. With each passing minute, I get more frightened for him."

"Let's check the cottage," Noah suggested, and they hurried down the drive toward the new teacher's house.

They had just reached the door when they heard a shout.

"Noah! Rachel! Any luck?" Charlotte said. She and

Abram Peachy joined them as they were about to enter the house.

"We checked the school, but he isn't there. We were about to see if he could have hidden inside when it got too late for him to find his way home again."

Rachel's gaze went to Abram Peachy, who looked ashen. "Abram—"

"We have to find him," the widower said.

"We will," Charlotte assured him and touched his arm briefly.

Noah went to insert the key into the lock, and the door pushed open at his touch. The four searchers looked at each other.

"Go ahead," Noah urged Abram.

The kindly older man nodded and entered with Charlotte close behind him. Noah and Rachel hung back.

"Shall we search the yard in the back of the house?" Rachel suggested, feeling helpless while waiting.

"Jacob?" she heard Abram call. "Jacob, son, if you're here, come to *Dat*. I won't be angry. I just want you safe at home."

Rachel heard Charlotte's voice. "Jacob, listen to your *dat*. He loves you. Please come out if you're here."

Noah and Rachel were rounding the house back toward the door when they heard a sudden jubilant cry.

"He's here!" Charlotte cried out to the two of them. "He was hiding in the bedroom. He's well." She went back inside to check on father and son.

"Praise the Lord," Rachel whispered.

"Amen," Noah whispered. He looked at her, and she saw him blink away tears.

"It was a *gut* idea to search here."

"And we weren't the only ones who thought of it," Rachel replied. She closed her eyes, listening to the sounds of the night, happy that a little boy was reunited with his father.

"We should get back," Rachel murmured, although she wasn't in any hurry to move.

"I'd like to see Jacob when he comes out," Noah said.

Rachel agreed. "Will Abram keep his word and not be angry with Jacob?"

"*Ja*. Abram is a man of his word, a *gut* man. And he is a father who just wanted his youngest son out of danger."

Charlotte came out of the cottage first. She beamed at them. "Now we will be able to sleep well tonight."

Abram followed her, carrying his son in his big, strong arms. He had tears of joy as he approached. "*Danki,*" he said in a choked voice.

Noah smiled in acknowledgment. "Jacob, boy, next time you want to play on the swings, ask one of us to take you."

"*Ja,* Noah," the little boy whispered. He looked as if he'd been through a lot. He still wore a frightened look until Abram tightened his hold on him.

"We'd best get back. Did ya walk?" Noah asked Charlotte.

"*Nay,* we went back to the house and got the carriage," Charlotte said.

Rachel saw then the small open buggy that Charlotte and Abram had taken from the Kings' barnyard.

"Ya can ride with Charlotte," Abram told Rachel.

"We'll enjoy the walk back to the Kings'," Noah said with a glance at Rachel, who nodded. "It's a nice night and it didn't take us long to get here."

Charlotte eyed her cousin in understanding. She said something softly to Abram, and then she, Abram and Jacob climbed into the courting buggy and with Jacob on Charlotte's lap, they headed out onto the road toward the dirt lane that would take them back to Aunt Mae and the others who would be waiting.

Rachel and Noah began to walk back. The night seemed alive with summer scents. The cricket chirps joined the croaking of frogs along a ditch by the roadway.

Rachel felt Noah's presence more keenly. She tried not to think of anything but returning to the house, but she couldn't help but be aware of Noah, who made her feel alive…and tingly…and afraid to put a name to her feelings.

Noah walked silently beside Rachel, keenly aware of her nearness. She looked appealing with the *kapp* upon her hair slightly askew. She had been disturbed from her sleep and no doubt dressed quickly. She appeared vulnerable and he couldn't keep his eyes off her.

She cut him a glance, and he averted his gaze. "It's so quiet," she said softly.

"Ja," he answered. "You can hear the frogs and crickets."

Distant cries of happiness interrupted the night: Rachel and Noah exchanged grins. Abram and Charlotte must have arrived with Jacob.

"I imagine you'd rather have ridden with Charlotte," Rachel murmured.

"Nay, I'm content enough to walk back. It's a nice night."

Rachel's stomach fluttered. "It was thoughtful of you to walk back with me."

Noah stopped to stare at her. "There was nothing thoughtful about it, Rachel. I wanted to walk back with you."

And her heart started to thump hard. She didn't know

what to say, didn't know how to answer. She remained silent as she accompanied him back to her aunt and uncle's farm.

As they approached the farm, Rachel began to hurry. It wasn't that she didn't want to spend time in Noah's company, but she was more confused than ever about her feelings for him.

She tripped and Noah caught her before she fell. He held her a few seconds, and Rachel stared up at him, breathing hard.

"Danki," she whispered.

He seemed to struggle with something. "We should go," he said huskily.

Rachel nodded as they continued through the night back to the King farm.

Aunt Mae, Charlotte and Nancy were fussing over Jacob as Rachel and Noah approached.

The child looked grateful to be back within sight of his father.

"I should get home," Abram said.

"Nay," Aunt Mae insisted, "you must stay the night with us. Mary Elizabeth, David, John and Ruthie are at Sarah's, *ja?*" The widower nodded. "No sense going there to wake up the children," she continued. "Eli will head home to let Sarah know that Jacob is all right. Jacob can sleep with Joshua and John. I can make a bed for ya down in the parlor."

"Ja, stay," Charlotte urged.

Abram nodded. "I am tired, and it is late. As long as the others know that Jacob is fine and we'll be spending the night here."

"Jacob." Charlotte held out her hand, and the little boy took it. "Come with me."

"Dat?"

Abram reached down to pick up his son, gave him a hug before setting him down. "Go along with Charlotte, now."

Charlotte's gaze met Abram's over Jacob's head as the boy took the young woman's hand.

"I'll get bedding for Abram," Rachel offered, noting the look of warmth between her cousin and the widower. She shot Noah a glance. Did he notice that something was happening between Charlotte and Abram? Or was she mistaken?

Noah didn't seem in the least concerned.

"Is there anything I can do to help?" Noah asked as he followed everyone inside.

"You have done more than enough, Noah," she heard Abram answer as she entered the house to find the linen cabinet.

Noah allowed his gaze to linger on Rachel as she hurried upstairs. If not for the worrisome circumstances of the evening's search, it would have been a wonderful night spent in Rachel's company. He had been focused on finding Jacob, but he had also enjoyed the closeness brought on by the dark night during the walk back. Something was happening between them. He sensed that she felt it, too.

"I guess we should head home, son," Samuel said, interrupting Noah's thoughts. "We need to tell your *mam* and brothers that Jacob is found and they can stop looking."

Rachel returned with a pillow and a quilt. Her gaze caught Noah's briefly as she left the room to make up Abram's bed.

"Is anyone hungry?" Amos asked. "Noah? Samuel?"

"*Nay,* Amos," Samuel said.

Samuel, Amos and Abram talked about the fright they'd suffered and the blessings of the good Lord in finding Jacob so quickly.

"But I wouldn't mind a muffin or piece of cake," Noah said to Rachel as she entered the room.

"I'll find something for ya in the *kiche*," she said.

He trailed behind her toward the kitchen pantry. "Got any chocolate cake or pie left?"

Rachel chuckled. "I'm sure there is some of each."

Noah waited while Rachel cut him two pieces of cake and set them along with two blueberry muffins on a plate for him to take home.

She smiled. "In case Samuel is hungry when you get home." She stopped as if to listen, and he heard the sound of horse hooves and turning wheels on dirt in the yard near the house. "Your *dat* has brought the wagon around," Rachel said.

Noah nodded. Using two fingers, he sneaked a piece of cake and placed it between his lips. "I like chocolate."

"I couldn't tell," Rachel replied, her eyes twinkling.

"Noah!" Samuel called.

"Coming, *Dat*." His brown eyes warmed as they settled on Rachel. "I will enjoy the cake and muffin."

Rachel nodded as she followed Noah through the house and front door. "Enjoy the desserts, but offer some to your *dat*." She stood on the porch, watching as Noah descended the steps.

Suddenly, he turned to capture her gaze. "I'll see you soon," he promised.

Her heart fluttered within her chest. "You'd better go. Your *dat* is waiting."

"Some things are worth making one wait," Noah returned with a smile, which sent Rachel's pulse racing. He left then to join his father on the wagon.

Amos and Mae saw them off with Rachel watching from a distance. It had been an unusual evening, she thought. Who could have imagined that they would be out looking for a child so late at night?

No blame would be given this night. Jacob had disappeared and was found, that was all that mattered to anyone, including the boy's father.

"Sleep in for a while in the morning," Aunt Mae told Rachel as they returned to the house and prepared to ascend the stairs.

Rachel nodded. She looked up as her cousin appeared at the top of the stairs. "Jacob is sleeping," Charlotte said. She looked concerned as she continued, "How is Abram?"

"He is glad now that he has his boy again. He has just gone to bed," Aunt Mae answered from behind Rachel. "You should all sleep in tomorrow. There will be plenty of time to get our chores done. Nancy?"

"Mam?" Nancy came in from outside and went to the bottom of the stairs.

Mae smiled at her daughter. "Head on up to sleep, now."

Nancy nodded. *"Gut* night, *Mam—Dat,"* she added as Amos joined Mae.

Then she headed up to bed, with Rachel following closely.

"Mam." Charlotte paused on the stairs and faced her mother. "Abram need anything?"

Mae smiled. "Abram has everything he needs for now."

Satisfied, Charlotte continued upstairs. Rachel and Nancy were ready for bed when she joined them in their room.

"What a frightening night," Rachel said softly as she climbed into bed.

"Ja," Charlotte replied. "Terrifying. Thank the Lord that Jacob was found."

"Amen," Nancy murmured sleepily, and then a couple of seconds later, she said, "I'm tired."

"We should get to sleep," Charlotte said, snuggling down under the covers. "I think *Mam* forgot that we'll have two extra mouths to feed in the morning."

Chapter Ten

Despite her aunt's urging to sleep in, Rachel was up at the crack of dawn. Nancy, she saw, slept on. Charlotte was already out of bed and downstairs.

Rachel dressed and went down to find Aunt Mae and Charlotte fixing breakfast for Uncle Amos, Abram and little Jacob.

"Looks to be a fine day," Rachel greeted as she entered the kitchen.

"Ja." Amos flashed her a smile. "Ya look well rested."

"I am." She pitched in to bring food to the table.

Little Jacob waited while Charlotte fixed him a plate of eggs, bacon and a freshly baked biscuit. He grabbed a fork and started to dig in.

"Jacob," his father scolded softly, "we need to thank the good Lord."

The boy looked at Abram, nodded and put down the fork.

When all of the breakfast food had been placed on the table, Aunt Mae, Charlotte, Rachel and Nancy, who had just joined them, stood and bowed their heads.

Amos, Jacob and Rachel's cousins John and Joshua bowed their heads and waited patiently while Abram led them in a prayer of thanks to the Lord God.

"Lord, You have blessed us with many things…this fine food Mae has placed before us…the love of family and friends…and helping us to find my Jacob." He was silent a moment as if overcome with emotion. Rachel chanced a look and saw that he was.

"You have given us much and we thank You for it. Help us to continue to do Your will. In this, we pray."

"Amen," everyone said.

Abram gave his son an approving look. "Eat, Jacob." And the boy was only too happy to oblige as he ate with a gusto that made his elders chuckle even while Charlotte urged him to slow down so that he didn't get a bellyache.

Rachel helped to clean up after the meal, and then she accompanied Charlotte, Abram and Jacob to the Peachy farm. They arrived to find Sarah with Jacob's brothers and sisters. The children ran toward Jacob when they saw him, firing several questions at once.

Jacob answered one or two while Abram watched silently until finally he spoke up. "Mary Elizabeth, did you feed the chickens?"

"*Nay, Dat.* We only just arrived."

His expression soft, he said, "Go feed them, then." His daughter nodded and then scurried away. He turned toward his son. "Nathaniel—"

"Going to let out the horses now, *Dat.*"

Abram nodded approvingly.

"Rachel and I will milk the cows," Charlotte said, and without waiting for an answer, she waved her cousin toward the barn to get the job done.

Rachel didn't mind doing the milking. It was a chore

she did happily. There was something calming about the simple task…the scent of the barn…the warmth of the cow's teats as she gently squeezed and pulled rhythmically…the heifer's low, pleasurable mooing as her milk supply was relieved.

Abram had four milk cows. Rachel and Charlotte each milked two and transported the milk from their stainless steel buckets into a large gas-refrigerated storage can. They would bring enough into the house for the family's use. The rest would stay cold and ready for sale for the community residents and the occasional English dairy farm looking for any extra fresh milk to pasteurize.

As the young women picked up their stools, Charlotte said, "We can stop at the house to see if anything needs doing before we head home."

Everything was being taken care of back at the house. Cousin Sarah had stayed to help, and the kitchen was spotless as the young women entered.

"Where is Abram?" Charlotte brushed stray strands of blond hair from her face, tucking them under her *kapp,* as she entered the house.

"He has gone out into the fields." Sarah smiled. "He took Jacob with him."

"Afraid to let him out of his sight," Rachel suggested.

Charlotte nodded. "Are you going to stay awhile?" she asked her older sister.

"I told Abram I'd stay until he got back. You can go home. I'm sure *Mam* has things for you to do."

"She does. Where are the girls?" Charlotte approached the stove where her sister stirred a pot of simmering chicken stock.

"Upstairs in their room." Sarah briefly gestured over

her shoulder toward the front of the house before she added a bowl of cut carrots to the stock.

"I'll just say goodbye," she told Rachel, "and then we'll leave."

Rachel would have offered to come, but she had the feeling that Charlotte wanted to see the children alone. She turned to find a thoughtful look in Sarah's expression. Perhaps Charlotte's behavior seemed strange even to her sister.

"Rachel! Noah is here to take us to Miller's!"

"Coming, Charlotte!" Rachel hurried to get ready for the trip into town. It had been a long time since she'd been shopping. Today Charlotte, Noah, Joshua and she would be heading to not only Miller's but to other stores before stopping for ice cream. She had looked forward to the trip since they first spoke about it weeks ago.

She wanted to get a few things for the classroom and her new house. Her new church district had given her money to buy what she needed. Perhaps she'd purchase some linens and kitchen utensils....

And she was pleased that it was Noah who would be taking them.

With her *kapp* set neatly on her hair and her apron secured over her royal-blue dress, Rachel hurried downstairs to join the others. She wore black shoes since she would be traveling among the English. If she'd stayed home, she would have gone barefoot because of the warm, sunny day.

Charlotte stood talking with Noah on the front porch when Rachel appeared.

"Rachel, I won't be able to go," she said. "Here—" She handed her Aunt Mae's list. "You can handle the shopping, can't you?"

"Ja." Rachel frowned as she accepted the sheet of paper. "But I thought you were going, too."

"That was my plan," her cousin said, looking unconcerned, "but I just found that Grandma Emma needs me to help her in the house. She's feeling poorly and wants me to spend the day with her."

Ride into town with Noah but without Charlotte? Rachel felt a bit discomfited. Was it proper?

"Joshua will be going," Charlotte said, as if she'd read Rachel's mind. "He wants his ice cream."

Aunt Mae joined them on the front porch, wiping her hands on her quilted cooking apron. "All set?" she asked.

Joshua burst out of the house, and Charlotte grabbed hold of her brother and ruffled his hair. "I told Rachel that I'll be staying to help Grandma Emma today."

Aunt Mae nodded as if she'd known about the arrangement. "Would you mind taking John? He may want to go. Joshua?"

"Mam?" He squirmed out of his sister's grasp.

"Go find your brother and ask him if he wants to go into town with Noah and Rachel." Mae eyed her youngest son's tousled hair. "And get your hat! You'll not leave the house without your head properly covered."

As if to tease his older sister, Joshua skirted an area far from Charlotte before he ran to do his mother's bidding.

"You want me to stay and help?" Rachel offered, feeling that she should.

"Nay, child. You go into town. I need someone who knows how to cook to do my food shopping. You've been working hard since you came to Happiness. Go and enjoy your ice cream."

Wearing a straw hat on newly combed hair, Joshua appeared moments later with his older brother.

"We're going for ice cream?" John put on his banded straw hat as he approached.

"Ja." Noah pulled dollar bills out of his pants pocket.

"I'll go!" His excitement waned as he suddenly gave his mother a little-boy look. "You sure *Dat* won't mind?"

"Nay, he'll be fine with it. You go, son, and have a nice time in town."

"I'll be sure to get everything on your list," Rachel promised.

"Don't forget the raised doughnut mix," Aunt Mae urged, "and have a wonderful time."

Noah helped Rachel onto the front seat of the wagon, while the two King boys climbed into the back. Rachel felt the dip and sway of the vehicle as Noah climbed on board and sat next to her.

Aunt Mae came off the porch and shielded her eyes from the sunlight with her right hand. "Noah, mind you bring them home before supper time."

"I will, Aunt Mae." He grinned at her as he picked up the reins. "Want any candy?"

Mae's eyes lit up with delight. "Licorice," she said.

"Licorice it is," Noah replied with a grin, and then they were off on an adventure into town for shopping and fun.

Rachel was silent as Noah guided the horse-drawn wagon down the lane and then left onto the paved road. Behind them, Joshua and John teased and taunted one another.

"I can eat more ice cream than you!" Joshua said.

"I'm bigger. I can eat more." John pushed down the rim of his brother's hat and Joshua tilted back his head to look up at him and said, "Can*not*. I may be little but I've got a bigger hunger than you!"

The exchange between them continued until their claims and excuses had become so funny that they laughed uproariously. Rachel and Noah flashed each other grins before they too succumbed to laughter.

"John, Joshua," Noah said when the hilarity had died down. "I know someone who can eat more than the both of you put together."

"Who?" John asked.

"Rachel!"

Her eyes widening, Rachel looked shocked. "Noah Lapp, you know that's probably true!"

Which was the last thing anyone expected her to say and everyone laughed again merrily as they traveled down the road on the beautiful, sunny day in Happiness, Pennsylvania.

They reached Miller's Store first. Rachel brought in her aunt's list, and with Noah's help, she was able to gather and purchase all the requested supplies quickly.

John and Joshua wandered about the shop, exclaiming about the cookies and candy for sale.

"All done, boys," Rachel announced. "Time to go. You want to try to out-eat me in ice cream, *ja?*"

Noah took some of her purchases, set them in the rear of the wagon, and then helped her to climb up onto the seat.

"Did you get everything you needed?"

"For Aunt Mae, *ja,*" Rachel said. "Among other things, I purchased two bags of doughnut mix for her." She straightened her skirt over her legs. "I had hoped to find a few things for the house."

"I know where you can get some household items. Shall we head there next?"

"Will they have linens and cookware?"

Noah nodded. "And fabric and many other household goods."

"That would be helpful," she said. "I would like that."

Noah took her to a small Amish shop located on a back road just outside of Happiness. He guided the horse onto the drive that led to a farmhouse and reined in by a small white outbuilding. He climbed down and roped the leathers around a hitching post.

"Yoder's General Store," Noah announced with a sweep of his arm.

Joshua and John scurried down from the back of the wagon. "May we go up to the house to see if Henry is there?"

"Don't be long. We'll have to be on our way soon if we are to finish shopping and eat our ice cream." Noah gestured toward the door of the store. "It may not look like much outside, but Margaret has a lot to offer. She can help you with whatever you need. If you don't see it in the store, she can get it for you." He held open the door for her. "Henry is Margaret and Harry's nine-year-old son."

"Noah, this is a nice surprise," Margaret said.

"I brought our new schoolteacher."

Rachel smiled. "Noah tells me you can help me find what I need for the new teacher's cottage."

Margaret returned her smile as she glanced back and forth between Rachel and Noah.

Rachel had made a list of things she needed before she could move in. "Sheets, towels…and do you have a good stockpot?" She read off several more items she would need after school started.

Rachel bought several items on her list and then ordered a couple from Margaret. "I appreciate your help."

"Let me know if there is anything else you might need."

The door burst open and Joshua, John and a third towheaded boy ran inside the store.

"Mam!" cried the boy Rachel decided must be Henry. "They're going for ice cream. Can we go, too?"

"Not today, Henry. I'll take you myself tomorrow."

Henry tried to hide his disappointment, but failed.

"Would you like me to take him and then bring him home?" Noah offered.

Margaret opened her mouth as if ready to decline. Rachel saw her study her son's eager expression, and she watched as Margaret relented.

"I'm sure Henry would enjoy that." Margaret reached into a jar behind the counter and came up with a few dollars. "Enjoy the ice cream on me."

Noah held up a hand. "That's not necessary. We're happy to buy Henry's."

Margaret hesitated, but then seemed to read something in Noah's features. "All right. *Danki.*"

"Come on, boys, let's get some ice cream!"

Rachel spoke briefly with Margaret about her order, and then she walked with Noah to join the excited young boys.

They drove toward the ice cream store, but then Noah pulled into the parking area of a local restaurant.

"I think we need to have a meal before ice cream," Noah said.

"Gut idea," Rachel agreed.

The boys weren't as enthusiastic. "Dinner," Joshua complained.

"How about a hamburger?" Noah suggested.

John's and Henry's eyes lit up. *"Ja!* Hamburgers!" they chorused, and Joshua joined in.

Noah hitched the horse to a post before he, Rachel and the three now-eager boys entered the restaurant. They were taken immediately to a table.

Noah glanced at each one of them. "All having the same?" The boys nodded. "Five burgers and fries," he said with a grin to the waitress.

"Something to drink?" the Englisher said.

"Three milks and two iced teas," Noah replied and was happy to see Rachel's nod of approval.

Seated across from Rachel, Noah studied her and liked what he saw. She chatted with the three boys, increasing their enthusiasm for the meal to come and the ice cream to follow soon after.

He felt a tightening in his stomach as Rachel flashed him a smile. She seemed relaxed and happy, and he was pleased that the first moments of tension between them, when she'd learned that they'd be going into town without Charlotte, had passed. If she was uncomfortable now, she didn't show it.

It wasn't long before the food arrived. John grabbed a bottle of ketchup and poured it liberally under the top of his hamburger bun and onto his plate for his fries.

The conversation was fun and teasing as Rachel and Noah watched three young boys enjoy their lunch.

Rachel was conscious of Noah's eyes on her whenever she wasn't looking at him. His glance made her feel flushed. She turned quickly to catch him staring and raised her eyebrows. Noah chuckled and handed her one of his fries, which she promptly popped into her mouth.

When they were done eating their burgers, they left the restaurant for the ice cream parlor. Everyone ordered a different flavor of ice cream cone. Rachel loved chocolate-chip-mint ice cream, while Noah liked rocky road. The two older boys tried unusual flavors like strawberry fudge ripple and banana crunch moon pie. Joshua was happy with a chocolate ice cream cone dipped in a chocolate candy shell.

They stood out in the warm sunshine, licking their cones quickly so that the melting ice cream wouldn't make a mess. They had just finished eating and climbed back into the buggy when Noah gestured toward the western sky.

"It looks like it's going to rain."

Rachel studied the darkening sky. "It appears black enough to storm. We'd better get Henry home and then head home ourselves before the rain hits."

Noah turned to the boys in the back of the wagon. "We're going to take Henry home."

"I liked the hamburger and ice cream, Noah," Henry said with a grin. His straw hat was slightly askew and his face was streaked with strawberry and chocolate.

"I'm glad you enjoyed it, Henry." Noah flicked the leathers and guided the horse onto the road.

"We did, too, Noah," Joshua said. "This has been the best day ever."

Rachel turned back to smile at him. "You're easy to please, cousin," she said. She reached out to tug his hat brim down over his eyes. Joshua snickered and pushed it back so that he could see again.

"John," Rachel said, "are you glad you came?"

"*Ja,* it was a *gut* day, all in all. I'm glad *Dat* let me out of my afternoon chores."

It wasn't long until they reached Henry's home. They found Margaret where they last saw her in the little shop. She had customers, William and Josie Mast and their daughter Ellen. The family was leaving as the town adventurers came in. "Afternoon, Noah," William greeted.

"*Gut* to see you, William, Josie." Noah pulled one of their daughter's *kapp* strings. "And how is Ellen today?"

The girl giggled. "Fine, Noah. *Mam* bought me candy."

Candy! Noah thought, recalling his promise to bring licorice to Mae. When the Masts had left, Noah turned to Margaret. "Do you have any licorice?"

"Aunt Mae!" Rachel exclaimed, and Noah nodded.

"Hard licorice or soft?"

"Soft," Noah decided, and Margaret scooped fresh licorice from a jar into a paper bag and handed it to him.

"How much do I owe you?"

"Zero cents."

"Margaret…" Noah narrowed his gaze and tilted his head, and Rachel thought he looked delightful.

"You bought my Henry lunch and ice cream," the shopkeeper said. "The least I can do is pay for the licorice."

Noah relented with a smile. "The candy is for Mae King."

"Please give her my regards," Margaret said.

There was a sudden low rumble of thunder. "We'd better get moving," Rachel said as she went to the door to look outside. "The storm is on its way."

"Let's go. John? Joshua? Back to the buggy! I've got to get you home."

A second distant rumble of thunder convinced the boys to hurry to the wagon, where there would be little protection if the storm hit before they got home.

Old Bess rose to the occasion, taking them quickly to the King farm and into the yard.

John helped Noah to unload the supplies and carry them into the house. Aunt Mae came from around the outside of the house with a basket of air-dried laundry.

"You're home in the nick of time," Aunt Mae said. "Noah, would you like to stay for supper? You can ride out the storm with us."

"I'd better go now, Aunt Mae. *Mam* will be worried, and it looks like the weather may take a while to clear."

The others went inside, and Rachel turned to Noah. "I had a lovely time today."

"I enjoyed our day together, too."

"The food was delicious."

The corners of his mouth tilted upward. "And the company?"

"The boys were entertaining," she admitted.

"And me?" he asked, and Rachel thought she detected a serious note beneath his banter.

"You are a skillful driver and a *gut* sport. I had fun spending the day with you."

His body seemed to sigh with relief. Studying him, Rachel had the strongest urge to touch his face, to trace his eyebrows…his nose…and the shape of his mouth. Shocked, she stepped back and looked away.

"You should go before the storm hits," she urged.

Noah studied her, wondering why she suddenly looked upset. There was already a storm within him. His feelings for her were causing all sorts of sparks and thunder and rain inside.

"I will see you again soon, Rachel Hostetler."

"Be careful, Noah Lapp." To his surprise and hers, it appeared, she touched his arm and drew back quickly.

A third rumble of thunder and old Bess's uneasy neighing had Noah jumping into the wagon. With a wave, he turned the wagon around, and with a loud *yah,* he headed toward home.

Rachel watched the wagon grow smaller as Noah drove away.

Noah Lapp. What was it about him that had her forgetting for not only moments but for an entire day the pain of her broken relationship with Abraham?

She had thought Abraham a kind man, but Noah was kinder. She had been attracted to Abraham, but not as much as she felt drawn to Noah.

Abraham had seemed to enjoy her company; Noah gave her all of his attention and wanted hers. He didn't just enjoy her company; he appeared to revel in it.

Charlotte. She knew she should have waited until Charlotte could come. What was she doing mooning over Charlotte's friend?

She closed her eyes as she stood outside. "Dear Lord, help me to be strong and true to Your word. Protect me from myself, in this I pray. Amen."

She turned and entered the house, and wondered how she was going to face Charlotte when she felt so guilty for liking Noah.

Chapter Eleven

Rachel stood by the window, studying the storm clouds. As it turned out, they had reached home in plenty of time. The thunderstorm was moving slowly. The residents of the King farm had just finished a simple supper of eggs, toast and ham. Now they could hear the wind pick up, rattling against the windowpanes. Lightning streaked the evening sky, followed by a deep rolling rumble of thunder.

A lightning bolt zigzagged down to earth, creating a loud bang and pop.

"Did ya see that?" Rachel asked, her eyes widening.

"I did," Charlotte said. She had returned earlier with Grandma Emma and Grandpa Harley. With the imminent arrival of the storm, she said she didn't want them to be alone in their house, even though their residence was less than an acre away on the same property. "Will it ever rain?"

There'd been a lot of bright flashes and loud booms, but so far there had been no rain, although the sky remained dark and ominous.

"I hope it does." Rachel flinched as another bright

bolt fell to earth, creating a loud boom. "We need it. I'm afraid of what the storm will bring if it doesn't rain soon."

"It's an unusual summer storm." Charlotte left the window to sit at the kitchen table. "I've never seen anything like this."

"Me neither." Rachel flinched at a clap of thunder. "I was hoping that this wasn't your average thunderstorm."

"We do get bad storms, but it's the flooding that sometimes concerns us. Not so much here on the farm, but hours of heavy rain can wreak havoc in the stores and shops in Lancaster and nearby villages."

"You all right in here?" Aunt Mae entered the kitchen to see the supper dishes had been washed and put away. "I'm glad you brought your *grosselders* here, Charlotte. Grandma Emma is terribly bothered by the storm. She has been praying nonstop since the wind kicked up and the thunder grew louder."

"Where are John and Joshua?" Rachel asked. She wondered if they were frightened by the storm.

"They're upstairs in their room. They love the adventure of a thunderstorm."

"Not me," Rachel said.

"Nor me," Aunt Mae replied, surprising her. She took a plate of cookies from the kitchen worktable. "I'll see if these will cheer Grandma Emma. She does love her sweets."

"Like you enjoyed your licorice?" Charlotte teased.

Aunt Mae had gotten into the licorice as soon as Noah had given it to her. In fact, she and Uncle Amos had eaten all of it in one sitting. Was it any wonder that neither one of them had wanted much to eat for supper? They had been content with breakfast food for the late meal. It had worked well for everyone. Rachel had been full from dinner out and their ice cream treat, as had her two young cousins who'd shared the day with her and Noah. Charlotte had made her grandparents a late dinner so none of them wanted to eat, either. Only Nancy had been hungry enough to eat two biscuits with her eggs and ham. It had been a quick meal to fix and easy to clean up afterward, which suited everyone just fine.

A flash through the white window curtains. A startling crack. Rachel and Charlotte rushed to the window to see if anything in the yard had been hit.

Whatever was struck, it wasn't as close as it sounded. When the downpour of rain began minutes later, Rachel was relieved. If something had been hit, the rain would help put out any possible fire.

The rain didn't last long, although the sky remained dark. Rachel heard a bang and a rumble.

"John! Joshua!" Aunt Mae scolded up the stairs. "Stop jumping on the bed!"

"Ja, Mam," John called back.

Aunt Mae returned to the kitchen. "Those boys," she said, but the softness in her expression told how much she loved her sons. Rachel had seen the same love in Mae's eyes for her daughters…and for her—her niece.

The rain began again, a steady downpour that soaked the earth. The lightning and thunder continued, and Rachel went to the window to watch for a while before she joined her cousins at the table. "Shall we play cards?" Charlotte suggested.

Grandma Emma entered the kitchen. "I'll play," she said.

They played Dutch Blitz to while away the time until bed.

They heard pounding on the stairs. "John, stop running—" Aunt Mae began, but then she saw the boy's face. "What's wrong?"

"Come upstairs. Come see the fire!"

"Fire?" Aunt Mae hurried up the stairs behind her eldest son, followed by her daughters, niece and mother-in-law. There was a good view of the smoke from the windows in the boys' room.

The dark smoke lifted despite the rain, and the wind threatened to spread the fire, wherever that might be.

"I think that's Abram's farm," Charlotte said with concern.

The storm had started to move away. Thunder continued to rumble in the distance and they could see occasional flashes across the sky. The rain had stopped, and steam rose from the main road's warm macadam as the water evaporated.

"We'd better see if Amos wants to head over to the Peachy farm," Aunt Mae said. Turning from the window, she crossed the room and headed toward the stairs.

"Amos!" she called as she descended the stairs. "There's a fire. We think it may be at Abram's house."

Amos came out of the parlor, followed closely by his father. He turned to Harley. "*Dat,* do you want to come?"

"*Ja,* of course. Abram is a *gut* man, and if it's not Abram's farm, then it must be another brother's."

"*Dat,* I want to go," Charlotte said.

"Perhaps we should all go, in case we're needed."

No one could argue with that logic. They crowded into the family buggy and went on their way. The lane was wet, but the puddles were no obstacles.

"We should alert the Lapps," Mae suggested as the buggy bumped its way toward the paved road. "We may need the boys' help."

"Ja," Amos said. "And Samuel's. I pray that no one is injured."

Mae's gaze met Rachel's. "I pray so, too."

The Lapp buggy was at the edge of the road when Amos drove near. Samuel stuck his head out the side window. "You saw the fire?"

"Ja," Amos called back. "It looks like Abram's."

Samuel locked gazes with his friend. "Hope it's not the house."

Amos's eyes widened. "Let's go." He worked the gelding into a fast trot as he drove the buggy toward the Peachy farm. Samuel and his sons followed behind them.

Rachel knew that Noah was in the vehicle with his father, but she didn't turn around. As the buggy neared the farm, the rising tide of smoke brought fear to Rachel's heart. *Dear Lord, please help them,* she prayed silently.

"It's the barn!" Charlotte exclaimed as her father parked the buggy a safe distance away.

"The animals!" John shouted.

The scent of smoke was thick in the air as they climbed from the buggy and dispersed. Amos immediately ran toward the barn, as did the Lapp men. Abram was leading one of his horses as he came out of the burning structure. The horse was blindfolded, her face covered by one of Abram's shirts. Still, the animal was skittish, perhaps sensing danger in the scent of smoke from the fire. Abram spoke softly to her as he led the horse away from the barn and fire toward the back of the house.

Charlotte, Mae, Rachel and Nancy headed toward the house, where the children stood eyeing the fire with frightened eyes. Charlotte immediately hugged the two younger girls.

"Ruthie. Mary Elizabeth," she crooned. "It will be all right."

Ruthie raised tear-filled eyes to Charlotte. "We saw a flash and heard a terrible bang, and then the barn was on fire."

"*Dat* ran outside to get to the animals," Mary Elizabeth explained. "He got our cows out, and we didn't want him to go back inside, but he went in and brought out Mattie and Blackie, our horses. Nate and Jonas ran to help him. Jonas led the cows to pasture. Nate shooed the chickens away from the barn and across the yard."

Rachel knew that Jonas was Abram's oldest son, and she remembered Nate from his teasing escapade with his sister's bonnet. Her gaze met her cousin's over the children's heads.

"Where's Jacob?" Charlotte asked, glancing around with concern.

"He's upstairs," Mary Elizabeth said. "He wanted to go with *Dat,* but *Dat* wouldn't let him. He ran up to his room. He was upset that *Dat* didn't think him man enough to help."

Rachel saw her cousin's frown. "I'll check on him." She knew where the boys' room was located from having cleaned the house before the Sunday church service that been held at Abram's.

Jacob stood at the window, blinking back tears as he watched the scene unfolding outside.

"Jacob." Rachel approached to stand at the window beside him. "Your *dat* is fine. The animals are safe, and while the barn is lost, your house hasn't been touched. It's something to be thankful for."

"But the barn…"

"They will put out the fire," she murmured, watching the commotion outside. She caught a glimpse of Noah along with Uncle Amos and the other men carrying buckets of water, swatting at the fire with shovels, as they worked to quell the blaze. She said a silent prayer for a heavy downpour of rain.

Relief came in the form of the fire department from the nearest town. An English neighbor had seen the smoke and come over to help. He had placed a call to the fire department on his cell phone. Within minutes a fire truck entered the yard and the firefighters had their thick hoses trained on the burning structure with the water supply from a tanker truck.

"Let's go downstairs and see your *vadder*," Rachel suggested.

Jacob nodded and Rachel held out her hand. He accepted and they walked together down the steps to the main floor.

Charlotte was in the kitchen, fixing food and drink for those who had worked to put out the fire. She poured iced tea and set up a plate of muffins and biscuits with butter and jam.

"They'll be hungry and thirsty," she said softly, but Rachel could hear the tremor in her voice.

She saw that Charlotte had the help of her sister, who came out of a back room. "We should make more iced tea and perhaps lemonade," Nancy suggested as she joined them.

Rachel addressed both sisters. "Jacob and I will be outside."

Charlotte nodded. "Where's *Mam?*"

"I'll find out. She's probably on the front porch."

In the yard, Aunt Mae offered the men a basin of

water and soap to clean the soot off their faces and hands.

Rachel called back to let her cousins know. She stood behind Jacob with her hands on his shoulders as he stared at the barn. She followed the direction of his gaze and noted the devastation.

"It's all gone," the young boy said brokenheartedly.

"Ja." Rachel gave his shoulders a little squeeze. "But no one was hurt, nor were the animals. We have much to thank the good Lord for. Barns can be rebuilt, but family or horses cannot."

Jacob caught sight of Noah, who approached. "Have you seen my *dat?*" the little boy asked.

Noah hunkered down before the distraught boy. "Earlier. He's fine, Jacob. The last I saw him he was talking with the man from the fire department—*after* the fire was put out."

The headlights from the fire engines and the lanterns and lights that belonged to Amish church members lit up the yard in the front of the house.

Rachel's gaze locked with Noah's brown eyes briefly over Jacob's head. Feeling a sudden jolt to her midsection, she broke eye contact to search the yard and the newly soaked, smoldering barn. Her heart raced wildly as she looked for signs of Abram. "Jacob, I see him!" She pointed in Abram's direction.

Jacob caught sight of his *dat* and ran toward him. Rachel watched Jacob hug his father about the waist.

"Are you all right?" Noah asked her softly as he rose to his feet, drawing her attention.

She frowned as her eyes met his. "I should be asking you. You were the one near the fire."

The corners of his lips curved slightly. "Were you worried?"

"And if I was?"

He looked pleased. "It would be *gut* to know."

"I was worried. This is a terrible thing." Her gaze left his to settle on the men gathered near Aunt Mae. Charlotte came out onto the porch with plates of food and a pitcher of lemonade with cups. She lifted a hand to wave. Rachel waved back and turned to see Noah lowering his arm.

Noah wiped his forehead with the back of his hand, leaving a streak of dirt on his skin. Rachel raised her fingers to wipe away the dirt and dropped them before making contact. *What am I doing? This isn't appropriate behavior!*

"Rachel!" Aunt Mae called. "Will you bring clean water and fresh towels?"

"Coming, Aunt Mae!" Rachel glanced down and saw a small red mark on the back of Noah's hand. "You have a burn," she said with sympathy. "I'll get you some ointment."

Rachel left before Noah could respond, running inside to find a pot to fill with fresh water and to look for clean towels and another bar of soap. While she was inside, she searched through kitchen cabinets until she found some B&W Ointment, an Amish remedy for burns and wounds.

She handed Aunt Mae the supplies she needed and a man from the local fire department came up to the group with a first-aid kit. He offered to check anyone's injuries.

Rachel saw Noah and then hurried toward him, unscrewing the cap from the ointment as she ran. "Let me see your hand," she urged as she reached him. She held his hand within her fingers and carefully spread the burn ointment onto the tender, red skin.

She heard a sharp intake of breath and her gaze shot up to lock with his. But it wasn't pain in his eyes that she saw. It was something else…something she didn't recognize but that made her feel strange and tingly inside.

"That should help," she said as she put the cap back on the ointment.

"I appreciate it." He looked satisfied as he studied his hand.

"Keep it clean," she warned without meeting his gaze. She didn't hear his answer as she turned and hurried back toward the house. She caught a glimpse of her cousin Charlotte talking with Abram. Rachel noticed the way Charlotte leaned closer to the widower as they spoke, and she frowned.

What about Noah?

She glanced back, but Noah now stood with his father and brothers as they spoke with the English firefighters.

She had to speak with Charlotte and soon. Was Noah going to court Charlotte?

The next morning Rachel went downstairs to find Charlotte alone in the kitchen, pulling muffins out of the gas oven.

"Would you like a blueberry muffin?" she greeted Rachel with a quick smile in her direction.

"*Ja,* I would." Rachel went to a kitchen cabinet and took out plates. She reached for a glass. "Would you like something to drink?"

"Orange juice." Charlotte began to loosen the muffins from the tin and place them onto a porcelain platter.

"Where is everyone?" Rachel set plates and knives on the table.

"*Mam* and Nancy went to visit Grandma Emma. *Dat,*

John and Joshua are out in the fields." She placed a muffin on each dish. "It's just you and me for breakfast. The others ate earlier."

Have I overslept? Rachel wondered.

"*Dat* asked the boys to get up earlier this morning as they had a lot to do today. *Mam* and Nancy got up to feed them."

Rachel took the pitcher of juice out of the refrigerator, returning to pour each of them a glass. "Charlotte, may I ask you something?"

Charlotte sat down, broke apart her muffin and spread fresh, homemade butter over each piece. "*Ja,* of course."

"Alta Hershberger mentioned that you and Noah would be courting soon." Rachel hesitated as she carefully, methodically buttered her muffin. "But I saw you with Abram. It looked like you are more interested in him."

Charlotte paused in the act of taking a second bite. "I am," she said softly, almost as if she was embarrassed.

Rachel took a bite and chewed it thoroughly. She blinked, startled, as her cousin's words registered. "You are?"

"I like Abram Peachy," she confessed. "I like Noah, too, but as a friend and a brother. Not as someone to court or marry."

Rachel felt her jaw drop. "But what about Noah? What if he feels differently?"

Charlotte shrugged. "Noah will be fine. You don't need to worry about him. He is a *gut* man who will find someone to court and marry."

Rachel couldn't stop thinking about her cousin's words all that day and into the next. Was Charlotte right? Or would Noah be upset to learn that Charlotte liked Abram?

And why did *she* care? She and Noah were friends... nothing more. She liked him—it was true. She wasn't ready to have a sweetheart. Or was she?

Abraham Beiler. She fell asleep that night thinking of the man she'd thought she'd marry...recalling the accident and the pain of her recovery in the hospital... and afterward.

The next morning when she woke up, she had a headache. Thinking about the past made her sick to her stomach. Her injuries from the accident had been extensive. The doctor had told her it was possible that she might not be able to give birth.

How could she ever marry when she wasn't able to have children?

Straightening the bed linens in her cousins' room, Rachel blinked back tears.

She must be content to be a teacher, to enjoy children other than her own, to take joy in teaching them English, writing and mathematics.

She heard talking in the kitchen as she headed downstairs and entered the room.

"The barn raising will be held on Thursday. We've put an order in for the lumber, and it will be delivered Wednesday." Uncle Amos sat at the kitchen table, jotting down notes with a pencil.

"Rachel!" Aunt Mae smiled at her. "We need to prepare food for the workers who will be at the Peachy barn raising. I know you wanted to move into the cottage this weekend..."

"Abram needs a place to house his animals." Rachel smiled as she sat down across from her uncle. "The cottage can wait."

Chapter Twelve

The members of the church community in Happiness arrived at the Peachy farm early Thursday morning. The lumber had been delivered the previous day.

Rachel saw the stack of wood and pallets of roofing shingles not far from where the old barn had stood. Several friends and neighbors had worked the day after the fire to remove the charred remnants of the old barn. The land was now clean of debris and ready for new construction.

Men had already begun work on the walls when the King carriage parked in the yard. The sound of hammers and saws filled the air and mingled with the men's shouts and the cries from the youngest children at play.

Rachel carried food items into the house. Aunt Mae and Charlotte were already in the kitchen coordinating storage of refrigerated items and directing the women who came to help.

The scents of bread, fried chicken and chicken potpie filled the room as Charlotte opened the oven to check its contents. The Amish chicken potpie, different from the English version, was coming along nicely. Charlotte had put the chicken on to simmer yesterday, and then she'd added potatoes, carrots and celery, cooking them until it was time to add the homemade potpie noodles she'd made with a half cup of flour and an egg.

The kitchen smelled wonderful, and Rachel checked to see if there was anything to be done before returning outside to set the tables, some of which were under a huge shade tree. The workers had arrived at six in the morning. Food was prepared and ready for the men and boys doing the construction all day. Muffins and biscuits with butter and jelly along with eggs, ham and sausage were put out first. There were pitchers of water, iced tea and lemonade, and hot coffee inside the house for anyone who wanted it.

Rachel stood behind a table, ready to serve the men and boys who took a break to eat. Jedidiah, Samuel and Elijah Lapp came to her table for breakfast first. Jedidiah grinned as he approached.

"Eggs? Sausage?" she asked while picking up a heavy-duty paper plate and lifting the spoon in the tray of eggs.

"Biscuits with butter and jam," he said, and Rachel placed four biscuits on his plate along with pats of butter and a large spoonful of jam. She gave him the plate with a fork and knife. He thanked her and accepted the lemonade that Rachel poured for him.

She fed every one of the Lapp brothers who came to her table...except for Noah, who stayed away. There was no sign of him, and she felt disappointed.

She spied him hammering two-by-sixes together to form one of the longest wall sections of the barn. She watched in fascination as he called to the closest workers—Horseshoe Joe Zook and his two sons, Josiah and Peter, and the four men hefted the massive wall upright and braced it into place. Another group of men had constructed a sidewall, and they hefted up the section, securing it to the length that Noah and his group had braced. They nailed the two walls together in the corner and secured the end wall in the same manner at the main front section.

Rachel watched for a time until Nathaniel Peachy appeared before her, looking for something to eat.

"Nate, helping out today?" she asked with a smile. She picked up a plate and gestured toward the food.

"Eggs and sausage, please," he said. "And may I have a muffin?"

"Ja." She set a muffin of his choosing onto his plate. "Would ya like something to drink?"

"Iced tea."

And Rachel poured him a glass and then another one as she saw her cousin John approach, looking thirsty after working in the summer morning sun.

She was kept busy serving the workers and returning inside to replenish what was eaten. The day was warm but not stifling, and the men worked up an appetite as the time passed.

She still hadn't spoken with Noah since she'd come earlier that morning. He remained busy hammering, measuring or sawing wood. Everyone seemed eager to grab a quick bite to eat, except Noah.

There were three other tables on the lawn filled with food. Five tables with benches near the house provided places for the men to sit and eat. Nancy, Anna Zook and Sally Hershberger served food from a different table. Another seven tables for sitting were on the other side of the yard.

Rachel saw Jedidiah come back for more food. This time he went to Annie Zook's table, and she saw them chatting and grinning as Annie loaded up Jedidiah's plate.

The boys old enough to help went to Rachel's table more often than not. She smiled, served them and told them that the barn was coming along nicely. But Noah still hadn't come to her table. She saw him now and again as he kept busy working on the barn. She couldn't keep her gaze off him, and once when he turned and saw her, she quickly looked away.

Charlotte gave little attention to Noah, but with Abram she was eager to help. What was she doing? Rachel knew that her cousin preferred Abram, but why didn't she think of Noah's feelings? Was that why Noah stayed away? Because he'd looked over and seen the way Charlotte was ready with drink, plate and attention for Abram whenever he stopped to eat or quench his thirst?

She frowned as she saw the way Charlotte leaned into Abram. Did others notice the interaction between the two? Or was she the only one who knew how Charlotte felt because her cousin had told her?

It was almost noon and dinnertime. Rachel went back inside to see what she could do about bringing out the meal the workers and their families would most enjoy.

Rachel had made peach cobbler from Aunt Mae's canned peaches. It had turned out well, as had the bread pudding, zucchini bars and vanilla cream she'd cooked the day before.

The kitchen was a hive of activity as the women pulled food out of the refrigerator and set some of it onto the stove to heat.

Nancy entered the house from outside. "Is there more iced tea?"

"*Ja.* It's in the refrigerator. There is also a fresh batch cooling on the table."

Rachel glanced about the crowded kitchen and asked, "Is there anything I can do to help?" It seemed as if there were too many cooks in the kitchen already.

Aunt Mae came up to her. "Would you take this outside?" This was a bowl of chicken potpie, and it smelled delicious.

"Do we have raisin bread ready?" Rachel asked as she accepted the bowl.

"*Ja.* Alta is putting on the icing now."

Rachel went out and set down the chicken potpie. She made several trips to the house to carry out more food. She had just set down a platter of buttered noodles when she felt someone's presence. Expecting to see Jacob, who had come back to her table many times, she turned with a grin.

Her grin slipped away as Rachel saw Noah waiting patiently at her table.

"You're hungry." She picked up a plate, wondering why he'd chosen that moment to come.

"*Ja.* Extremely hungry." He grinned. "There were things I wanted to finish before I stopped to eat."

Rachel nodded as she gestured toward the array of food. Other selections had joined the chicken potpie, including corn pie, both of which were kept warm with the use of Sterno. Yeast rolls, pickles, chow-chow and marinated green-bean salad were accompanying sides. There was a variety of desserts, including zucchini bars made with chocolate and butterscotch chips with walnuts and cinnamon. Rachel's peach cobbler sat on the table, smelling scrumptious. Noah eyed all the food and made his selections. He took some chicken potpie, buttered noodles and corn pie with marinated green-bean salad. When his plate was full, he took a seat at a table nearest to Rachel's serving station.

Rachel turned and saw that he was studying her with glistening, unreadable eyes. He took his time, which was his right, since this was the first break he'd taken since six o'clock this morning and it was now almost one. When he was done, he returned to Rachel's table.

"Which dessert did you make?" he asked, rubbing his clean-shaven chin.

"Peach cobbler," she answered, expecting him to look disappointed.

"I'll have some of that, then." He looked around the table. "And that." He pointed toward the zucchini bars she'd made.

Startled, she stared at him. "How did you know I made them?"

He shrugged as he ran his hands down the length of his suspenders. "They look good." He bent close to the plate she handed him, inspecting the zucchini bar carefully. "Chocolate chips?"

"Ja," she murmured as she rearranged some of the desserts. When she looked at him again, she saw his grin. His happiness made her lips curve upward.

"Anything else?"

"Ja," he said seriously. "What else did you make?"

She laughed, believing him to be teasing, but he didn't join in. "What does it matter?" she asked.

"I've been waiting all morning to eat with you. You have your dinner yet?"

She shook her head. "I've been busy serving and bringing out more food."

"Sit down and have dessert with me?"

"What about Charlotte?" She waited with bated breath to hear his answer.

"Charlotte would rather spend the time with Abram."

"And that doesn't bother you?" Rachel felt her heart start to pump harder.

"*Nay.* I'd rather spend time with you, not Charlotte." He gestured toward the table where he'd eaten his meal. "Come. Fix a plate and join me."

"I don't know…"

"Please?" He looked boyishly appealing, but she saw him not as a boy but as a man about whom she couldn't stop thinking.

Rachel glanced around to see if anyone was watching. She grabbed a plate, took a piece of peach cobbler and sat down at the table across from him at one end. Men and women didn't usually eat together…not in gatherings for church Sunday meals or on visiting Sundays. But this was a barn raising and the atmosphere was somewhat festive, despite the hard work of hundreds of those within the Happiness and nearby Amish communities who had come to help. She wouldn't be sitting with him alone. Other folks soon joined their table, filling the length of their benches. No one noticed anything amiss with her sitting at Noah's table. Everyone chatted about the food, the work and the good Lord's will.

Soon, Rachel had finished her cobbler and stood. Noah rose silently, and after one last look in her direction, he went back to work on the barn.

By the end of the day, Abram had a well-constructed new barn built by family, friends and neighbors. It had been a good day, blessed by God and appreciated by all.

That night Rachel lay in bed, staring at the ceiling. Her cousins were asleep. She could hear the sound of their soft breathing as she recalled the day's events and the strange revelations.

Noah had no plans to court Charlotte. Rachel felt a burning in her stomach.

He likes me. She wasn't sure how she felt about it.

When she'd arrived back at the house, she'd found a letter in the post from her mother. Rachel had written to her only last week, telling her about the school, the cottage and her aunt, uncle and cousins.

In her reply, Henrietta Hostetler wrote that all was well in Millersburg. Her mother wrote that she was glad Rachel liked her new home in Happiness. She had news she didn't know if she should tell, but she felt Rachel should hear it first from her.

Abraham and Emma Beiler were expecting their first child.

Rachel had suffered mixed feelings when she'd read about the news. She'd reacted differently than she'd expected. She was no longer upset that Abraham had left her for Emma. When she thought about why, only one reason came to mind. *Noah.*

Rachel rose from bed and went to the window. It was a warm summer night, and with the windows open, she could hear the crickets…and the light stirring of a breeze in the trees and bushes.

Noah Lapp. She shouldn't like him, but she couldn't help herself. She must keep her distance, for his sake as well as hers. But whenever she thought of his smiling face, she could feel her resolve dwindling. Noah Lapp.

School would be starting soon, and she'd be moving into the cottage and getting ready for her students.

Noah Lapp. Her head said one thing, but her heart was telling her something else. *Stay away. Enjoy his company.* Head and heart were dueling, adding to her confusion.

She closed her eyes, blocking out the night for a moment, but Noah's face filled her mind, and she knew it was hopeless. She went back to bed, tried to relax, forget about the day, thought only of the times she'd spent in Noah's presence…the laughter they'd shared…the smiles…the looks.

Dear Lord, help me to do Your will. Give me the strength to accept what may happen.

During the week that followed, the temperature rose several notches. It was too hot to do much work, so the family sat on the front porch, trying to beat the heat with inactivity, lemonade and iced tea.

To Rachel's surprise, Noah came over to sit with them daily. He arrived in the morning and stayed until just before dinnertime, when he returned home to eat the meal with his family.

Rachel enjoyed those moments he was there. Sitting in the midst of her relatives, she could watch and listen to the conversations between family members and between Noah and Uncle Amos.

Noah sometimes returned in the afternoon with one of his brothers—occasionally Jedidiah, but more often than not his younger brother Jacob, which seemed to please Nancy.

The heat wave lasted a week and a half before breaking. Once the temperature dropped, everyone worked to get caught up on chores left undone, including Rachel, who went to the teacher's cottage to set things up the way she wanted.

The house was ready for her to move in. Her bed was in place and she had all the linens she needed to be comfortable.

She planned to move in the next day. Upon hearing Rachel's intent, Aunt Mae had urged her to accept Charlotte and Nancy's company for the first night or two after she'd taken residence.

Rachel didn't mind. Truth was, she wasn't sure how she felt about living alone, but she had been in her uncle's household long enough. She had things to do in the schoolhouse. It made good sense for her to be close enough that she didn't have to worry about rushing to get to school. She could rise, eat breakfast and walk down a short gravel driveway to open and ready the classroom.

She enjoyed her first night in the cottage with her cousins. Charlotte, Nancy and she giggled long into the night before finally falling asleep in the same room. Rachel and Charlotte slept in Rachel's double bed, while Nancy slept on a comfortable pallet made with a thick layer of quilts on the wooden floor right next to the bed.

They stayed for the first three nights after Rachel's move. During the second day, Noah and his brother Jacob appeared on Rachel's doorstep. Charlotte let them inside.

"Is everything working all right?" Noah asked, glancing about as if to see that all was in order.

"Fine. Everyone is *gut*," Charlotte said.

"Rachel," Noah greeted. "You like the bed? Is it comfortable?"

Rachel flushed. "*Ja*. Charlotte and I slept well last night."

"We just stopped by to see that all was in order. If you need anything, you know our house is not far."

Rachel nodded. She saw that Jacob and Nancy were grinning at each other. She controlled a little smile.

"Would you like breakfast?" Nancy asked.

"Ja—" Jacob began.

"Nay," Noah said simultaneously.

"We've got fresh cinnamon rolls." Charlotte held up a plate of the fresh-baked, newly iced cinnamon rolls. The aroma wafting from the treat smelled delicious.

Jacob and Noah exchanged looks. "Noah?"

Noah sighed and then smiled. "They look and smell wonderful. Do ya have enough?"

"We have another half dozen in the oven," Charlotte said, gesturing toward the kitchen table.

Rachel watched helplessly and with a secret thrill as Noah made himself comfortable in a chair next to Jacob's. Recalling her manners, she went to the stove and held up a metal coffee pot. "Would you like a cup?"

Noah held her glance as he nodded, and Rachel quickly turned to take cups out of the cabinet. Her face felt warm and her heart beat rapidly.

"I'll have a cup," Jacob said and Rachel nodded. As she carefully poured each brother a cup of coffee, Rachel found the moment she needed to gather her composure.

Her heart beat a rapid pace, but she believed she hid her reaction to Noah's presence.

Chapter Thirteen

What is the matter with me? Rachel wondered.

She set down the coffee cups and went to get the pitcher of cream out of the refrigerator and butter for anyone who wanted to spread some on a cinnamon bun.

It had been some time since Rachel had spoken with Noah, other than in the company of her relatives on the King family front porch.

"We're here to finish putting up Rachel's clothesline," Jacob said. He held up a roll of rope. The Lapp boys had put up the T-bars a day earlier.

Rachel nodded.

"I'll get started," Jacob said.

"I'll help," Nancy chimed in, and she hurried to follow Jacob out the rear door.

Charlotte, Noah and Rachel remained in the kitchen.

"Another cinnamon roll, Noah?" Charlotte asked cheerfully.

"*Nay.* But I wouldn't mind another cup of coffee."

"Rachel, I have to get over to Abram's to watch the children." Charlotte untied her patchwork apron. "Would you mind getting Noah's coffee?"

"Not at all," Rachel said, experiencing a sudden fluttering beneath her breast. She went to the stove for the coffeepot and brought it over to the table to pour Noah a second cup. While there, she poured some for herself.

The sugar was on the table. "More cream?" she asked as she returned to check the pitcher. She was conscious of the fact that she and Noah were suddenly alone. The flutter within her chest quickened.

Noah handed her the pitcher of cream. "There is enough."

Rachel poured in a small amount after she added a spoonful of sugar. She handed the pitcher back to him, for she'd noticed that he'd given her the cream first. She stirred her coffee and then glanced over at him. He was watching her, a slight smile playing about his lips.

"I appreciate the breakfast," he said, his warm brown eyes twinkling.

"Charlotte made the cinnamon rolls."

"But you made the icing," he said.

She frowned. "How did you know that?"

"You've got a bit of icing on your apron." He leaned toward her and lowered his voice. "The icing is the best part."

She felt an infusion of warmth. It wasn't appropriate for her to be alone with him, not when she was feeling this way. She stood and went to the sink to pour out the last of her coffee, which had tasted bitter to her. "Noah—"

"Ja?" Noah rose from his seat and approached. Rachel seemed skittish. Was she nervous around him? After the outing they'd shared and the search for little Jacob Peachy?

It was wonderful to see her. He wanted to spend more time with her, but he could tell that something was bothering her. Had she been hurt in the past? He liked her, and he'd thought that she liked him, but lately she seemed distant.

He wanted to court her. Should he tell her? Or would it only frighten her more? He could make himself helpful to her, ready to fix anything in the school or cottage. He could fetch her supplies or offer to take her into town again.

Rachel was startled to turn from the sink and find Noah right behind her. She glanced up at him, wondering why exactly he had come. He didn't need to enter the cottage to put up the clothesline. Unless he had wanted to see her....

Now that she knew he and Charlotte weren't interested in each other, she should feel relieved, even happy...but how could she when she was afraid to become involved? There was much he didn't know. She couldn't risk it...yet.

They stood in close proximity for a long moment, and the tension between them was thick and laced with a tinge of excitement...at least for Rachel.

She thought Noah was about to say something, but he must have thought better of it, for he withdrew a few steps.

"I'd better get outside to help Jacob with the line."

Without saying a word, Rachel nodded.

"You will tell me if there is anything that needs fixing?" Noah stood at the door with his hand on the knob.

"I will," she assured him, not able to meet his gaze.

"Sink is all right? Any doors squeaking or sticking? Shower work well?" He listed several things that must have concerned him.

"Everything is fine," she said quietly.

Noah smiled, and his genuine warmth radiated

across his features. "I hope you will be happy in your new home."

"It is wonderful. I will enjoy living here."

Then after a quick nod, Noah exited through the back door, and as he disappeared from view, Rachel went to stand in the doorway to catch another glimpse of him. She saw him approach his brother and Nancy, who were teasing each other, if their laughter was any indication. She watched Noah and Jacob exchange words, and then she continued to study Noah as he and his younger brother secured each length of line on the wooden T-bars, allowing plenty of room for her to hang her laundry.

A new washing machine would be delivered later this week. Until it came, she would rinse her clothes out in the sink or go to her aunt's to do laundry but return to hang her garments on her newly constructed clothesline.

As if he sensed that she was watching, Noah turned toward the house and waved.

She stepped outside and waved back. "It is a *gut* clothesline," she called across the yard.

He nodded and grinned, and then he left with his brother a few minutes later.

Noah was everywhere. She couldn't have ignored him if she'd wanted to, which she realized she honestly didn't. Still, Rachel did her best to discourage Noah Lapp's attention whenever he came to the schoolhouse—which was often—and whenever he visited the cottage, which was at least once every other day. And during church service and the meal afterward, Noah was always near…watching her…making her aware of his presence.

If something needed fixing at the school, he appeared

as if summoned. When the lock on the cottage's back door got stuck, he was there to reposition the lockset with hammer, chisel and screwdriver.

One morning after her cousins returned home, Rachel had awakened to find flowers on her front doorstep. Only one person came to mind when she saw the flowers…the same man who had picked wildflowers for her and Charlotte the first time she'd visited the schoolyard.

Sunday arrived and church service was held at Joseph and Miriam Zook's farm. Everyone came in their Sunday-best black, including the children, who behaved well during the service.

Rachel again noticed Noah's presence during the service and afterward during the meal, but he didn't approach to speak with her. She didn't know how she felt about that. She kept her distance, glanced over at him from time to time to see if he was watching, noticing her, but his attention had turned elsewhere. To her disappointment, he talked with everyone, it seemed, but her.

She ate, enjoyed the company of the community women. As usual, Alta Hershberger had a lot to say about many people, and while she listened politely, Miriam Zook didn't join in the discussion as she usually did. Rachel narrowed her gaze as she studied her. Was Miriam all right? She approached the woman when she had the opportunity to talk with her alone.

"Miriam?" she said softly. "Aren't you feeling well?"

Miriam smiled and regarded her with kindness in her gaze. "I am well, Rachel." She paused to instruct her daughters to put out the desserts. "Are you settling in at the cottage?"

"Ja," Rachel said, taking the hint that if something was bothering the woman, Miriam preferred to keep

it to herself. "It's a comfortable house. Have you been by to see it lately?"

"*Nay.* I meant to, but there was so much to do with my parents. *Mam* is not well. She just came home from the hospital. *Dat* had a hard time while she was gone. It is good that both are back home in the *grosselders'* house. It's been a worry."

Rachel felt instant compassion. "Is there anything I can do to help?"

Miriam smiled as she brushed crumbs off her apron. "You are a dear. We are doing better now. I appreciate your offer. If I need you, I'll let you know." She gestured to her daughter Annie to take the chocolate cake and shoofly pie. "Alta means well," Miriam said. "She is a *gut* God-loving woman. We all are curious about our friends and neighbors."

Rachel nodded. It was true. Wasn't that why *The Budget,* the Amish newspaper, was a popular read?

As Miriam continued to oversee the kitchen, Rachel grabbed a pan of blond brownies and rejoined the other women who were moving food on the tables outside.

She was thoughtful as she shifted plates and made room for the pan as well as the other desserts that Annie and her sister Barbara brought out for all to enjoy. *The Budget* had news from Amish communities all over the country. Neighbors reported everything from who was ailing from what to the weather, as well as deaths, births and any other news deemed reportable by someone in the community.

Rachel felt her stomach tighten as she recalled her accident. She knew it had been reported in the Amish newspaper. Not by her family, she knew, but by a neighbor. She hadn't realized at first. When Rachel was in the hospital, the outpouring of love and caring toward her had been tremendous. She'd received cards and letters from family and friends. It was when she began to receive mail from folks outside Millersburg that she had guessed. The fact disturbed her, at first, until she realized that no one knew the true extent of her injuries. They'd just learned that she'd been hurt seriously enough for family and friends to ask everyone to pray for her.

Katie Lapp and Noah came up to the table and Rachel shook off her mood. It was the first time Noah had approached her all day.

"The desserts look delicious," Katie said with a smile. "I believe my son would like a piece of the chocolate-chip chocolate loaf."

Rachel couldn't keep from grinning. "No surprise there." She cut him a slice, and as she handed him a plate, she locked gazes with him.

"Rachel," he said with a small smile.

Heart thumping hard, Rachel tore her gaze away to smile at his mother. "Would you like a piece?"

"A tiny slice for Hannah." Katie turned as one of her younger sons, Daniel, approached with Hannah on his hip. "Daniel, would you like dessert?"

Young Daniel's eyes lit up. "*Ja!* Got any peach pie?"

Rachel nodded and cut Hannah's piece of the loaf before she reached for the pie to cut Daniel a generous helping.

The young boy grinned his thanks and handed his sister over to his mother before taking his pie and fleeing to enjoy it at the men's table.

"You need your diaper changed, little one," Katie crooned to her daughter. "I'll be back for Hannah's dessert," she said to Rachel.

"I'll bring it to you in a few minutes, *Mam,*" Noah said.

Katie left and Noah and Rachel faced each other alone. There were people milling about the yard but it seemed to Rachel as if they were the only two people on the earth.

"I haven't spoken to you all day," Rachel said after a few seconds of silence.

Something flashed in Noah's expression. "Did ya miss me?"

Rachel eyed him carefully. *"Ja."* Her stomach tightened.

Noah's grin held pleased satisfaction. "You don't find my company annoying?"

"Nay!" She frowned. "Why would you think that?"

He shrugged. He looked wonderful in his Sunday best. His sandy-brown hair was neatly trimmed, his face clean-shaven. His white shirt, black vest and pants fit him well, she noticed. His eyes gleamed beneath his felt wide-brimmed hat.

"I was afraid you might have thought me too helpful." Noah broke off a small piece of chocolate loaf and ate it. Rachel watched fascinated as he chewed and swallowed.

When she realized that she was staring, Rachel quickly looked away.

"There is a singing tonight," Noah said.

Rachel nodded. It was church-service Sunday.

"Will you let me drive you home afterward?" He held his fork in midair, and several heartbeats passed as Rachel digested what Noah was asking. It was one thing to have him walk her across the yard at her aunt and uncle's farm. But the journey from the Zook house to the teacher's cottage was longer and would require more time alone with him…unless his brothers would be accompanying them.

"Jacob will be taking Nancy," he quickly added, as if he had read her mind.

Did she like Noah Lapp enough for him to consider her his sweetheart?

Ja, she thought. Hadn't she gone over this in her mind again and again?

"I will be happy to ride home with you this evening, Noah Lapp," she said quietly, for she wanted no one else to hear.

His features lit up and his grin widened. "I missed talking with you today, Rachel Hostetler."

"Me, too." She felt suddenly nervous, as if meeting him for the first time.

"I'd better take Hannah her dessert." Noah held out his plate for another helping, and Rachel laughed and sliced more chocolate loaf. "I will talk with you later," he said softly.

"I will see you later, Noah." Rachel watched him walk away with two plates of dessert, and the day suddenly seemed brighter…while the night loomed excitingly ahead.

Chapter Fourteen

The gathering at the Zooks' ended at eleven-thirty that night. Everyone had a wonderful time. This night the singing was held in the Zook home rather than outside or in the barn. Miriam and her younger children stayed in the kitchen to help with the food before the children retired upstairs. Joseph Zook, the head of the household, had gone to William Mast's house for a time before arriving home and joining his wife in the kitchen for a bite to eat before heading upstairs with her. Their daughters Annie and Barbara were at the singing along with their eldest son, Josiah.

Annie had confided to Rachel that her parents enjoyed hosting the singing for the young people. It reminded them of their days of courting when Annie's *vadder* had driven her *mudder* home.

Rachel liked hearing the story of the Zooks. Horseshoe Joe and Miriam obviously cared for each other still, and it was nice to see another example of a successful marriage.

Neither Noah nor she had joined the church yet. Most of the young people at the singing had not. Joining the church was the decision of the individual. The older young people could enjoy a time of *rumspringa* to help them decide. During *rumspringa,* young people could discover a taste of the English way of life. Amish elders were lenient about the actions of young people during *rumspringa,* sometimes ignoring when they heard a radio playing out in the yard or when one of their sons temporarily exchanged his Amish garments for English clothes for trips into town.

Their being lenient didn't mean they liked *rumspringa.* They tolerated it as long as their children's actions weren't destructive or didn't end in arrest. The Amish community felt it necessary for young people to test the waters of outside life to help them make the decision of whether or not to join the church. Once they joined the church, then they had to abide by the *Ordnung,* the rules set by the community. If they did not, they could be shunned or banned, a terrible fate for a member of the community. But if a teen decided not to join the church, he could leave and not be shunned, for it was only after one made the commitment to join the church and to God that the *Ordnung* took priority.

Noah stood outside by the wagon when Rachel exited the Zook farmhouse. He approached when he saw her.

"It is a nice night," he said. "It should be an easy ride home. I have the lantern for the trip." He held up the light. There were also lights on the back of the wagon to alert any automobiles of their presence on the roadway.

"Have you seen Jacob?" he asked.

"Still inside." Rachel looked over at the house. "Here they come now."

Jacob and Nancy walked outside together, chatting and smiling into each other's eyes. Elijah, Noah's other brother, followed behind them. Charlotte was accompanying him, but as friends, not as sweethearts, for Charlotte liked Abram Peachy and Elijah liked Rebekka Miller, who had been unable to come to this evening's singing. Jedidiah stayed behind at the Zooks'; he would ride home with Benjamin Mast. He wanted to spend a few more minutes with Annie.

Noah helped Rachel onto the front seat and then climbed up next to her while everyone else piled into the back.

Laughter and socializing went on in the back of the wagon. Noah and Rachel were quiet as Noah guided old Bess onto the road toward home. But it wasn't a tense quiet, more like a pleasurable silence during which she and Noah exchanged warm glances and smiles.

As they traveled away from the Zook farm, Rachel felt a light brush on her left hand and looked down as Noah clasped her fingers.

No one in the back had noticed. Once or twice, Charlotte had to remind the merrymakers to lower their voices, as it was late and people in the neighboring homes they passed wouldn't appreciate having their sleep disturbed. After each scolding, the voices would lower and the giggles would soften until someone said something to make them all forget and their laughter would ring out loudly and Charlotte would hush and scold them once again.

"Noah." Jacob leaned over the back of the front seat, and Rachel quickly removed her hand from Noah's. "How about we take a side trip?"

"A side trip?" Rachel asked. She met Noah's glance, which looked soft beneath his hat brim in the lantern light. His brother's words made him frown. He obviously didn't care for Jacob's idea.

"*Nay,* brother," he replied. "*Mam* will be wondering where we are."

Jacob made a face. "*Ja,* I suppose she will be." He seemed to think for a moment before he said, "We can go another night!"

Noah shrugged. "It's possible," he said and then didn't say anything more.

Jacob turned back to the others, and the group continued to enjoy the ride, although they were disappointed that the night would soon end.

They arrived at the King farm, and Jacob climbed out of the wagon and helped Nancy to alight. Elijah in turn helped Charlotte. Noah and Rachel sat in the front seat for a while longer.

The silence was peaceful, but it seemed as if there were things to be said, only neither was speaking.

"It's late," Rachel finally said.

Noah nodded and turned to face her. "Rachel…"

"*Ja?*" She looked uneasy.

He studied her face, her brown eyes, her pink lips. "I'd like to court you." He saw her eyes widen.

"Noah…"

"I like you. You like me." He watched her and saw the truth in her expression. "We can enjoy each other's company."

"I don't know if I'm ready," Rachel whispered, although her heart was saying *ja, ja!*

"Ready," he murmured. "Rachel, did someone hurt you?"

She drew a long breath and inclined her head.

"You want to tell me about it?"

She shook her head vigorously. She wasn't yet able to discuss her former betrothed, the accident and Abraham's decision to marry her best friend.

Noah was studying her. Rachel tried to smile but failed miserably.

"I don't want to push you," he said, "but will you think about it?"

"*Ja,* I will think about it," she said softly.

"You aren't against the idea?" His expression was solemn.

She smiled, a genuine smile. "*Nay,* Noah, I'm not. I do like you, only…"

"You're not sure you're ready to court anyone?"

Her look was his answer. He grinned. It wasn't that she had a problem with him; the problem lay in her past, whatever that was.

"Will you meet me in the schoolyard tomorrow night?"

Close to the cottage, but out in the open, she thought. "What time?"

"After supper…about eight o'clock?"

She inhaled sharply. "I'll be there."

"I had a nice time tonight," he said.

She regarded him with warmth. "Me, too."

Jacob and Elijah were nearing the wagon. "Time to take you home."

Noah's brothers climbed into the back, and Noah guided old Bess back down the lane and onto the road toward the cottage where Rachel now lived.

Noah climbed down and assisted Rachel from the wagon seat. He walked her to her door, and she was conscious of the fact that his brothers were near, watching. He must have been aware of them also, for he spoke softly after he'd opened the door for her.

"I'll see you soon, Rachel Hostetler."

"See you soon," she echoed.

He entered before her, checking the house to make

sure all was well. He allowed her to go inside once he knew that she'd be safe.

"*Gut* night." He touched her hand.

She laced her fingers through his briefly before pulling her hand away. "Until tomorrow," she said and then went inside the house and watched from the doorway as he rejoined his brothers. After one last look, he drove the wagon away, and Rachel shut the door and locked it behind her before heading to her bedroom, where she thought of the day, the night and her next meeting with Noah.

He wants to court me.

She was thrilled; she was excited. But she couldn't be his sweetheart. The accident...

Or could she? The doctors hadn't been sure. What if they were wrong and she *was* able to have children?

Tomorrow night she would meet him. She felt a wild little thrill.

She made sure both doors and all the windows were locked except for the one room where she needed fresh air—her bedroom. Still, she opened that sash from the top and not the bottom, and put a chair piled with books beneath the window. If someone tried to enter through the open window, she would know about it.

She smiled as she put on her night garment. After brushing her hair, she climbed into bed. *Tomorrow will come soon enough. It is time for sleep.* Morning would come quickly, and there were things to be done in the schoolhouse...and she'd offered to help Aunt Mae with the baking.

Her last happy thought before she fell asleep was of Noah's excited expression when she'd agreed to meet him in the schoolyard.

* * *

Noah was standing by the swing set when Rachel entered the schoolyard. Her heart leaped at the sight of him. He looked wonderful in a green shirt with his triblend pants held up by suspenders. His wide-brimmed banded straw hat was pushed back to reveal the look in his eyes as she approached. Her heart started to pound hard.

"Rachel," he said with a formal nod, but his gaze was anything but formal.

"Noah." She glanced about the schoolyard and lane. "Did you walk?"

"*Nay.* I took the only buggy that was available." He gestured beyond the yard to where he'd tied up the horse. He had brought the single-bench courting buggy. "I don't suppose you'd like to go for a ride?"

Rachel eyed the buggy and then turned her gaze onto Noah. She trusted him. Hadn't he saved her when she was clinging for dear life on the runaway buggy?

The mare was Janey, a gentle soul who heeded Noah's commands.

"I'll go for a ride."

Noah felt a sudden lightening within. Rachel must trust him to agree to take a ride in the courting buggy. Not that they were officially courting yet. If he had his way, he'd be courting her soon, but he would go slowly. He didn't want to frighten her. He'd go slowly as long as he could.

He held out a hand and she accepted his help as she climbed into the buggy. The buggy moved under her weight, but Rachel smiled as she settled down onto the seat.

Noah climbed up to sit beside her. "You ready?" he asked softly.

She nodded as she straightened her skirt over her legs. "Where are we going?"

"We can travel down the paved main road a little or we can continue down this dirt lane, past the cottage and onto Lapp land."

It was light, but darkness would be descending soon. She preferred the farm lane rather than the road. She didn't trust the cars that might speed past—or the drivers who might not see them. "Your land," she said.

"Onto our farm we'll go then," he said, pleased at her response.

A light rain had dampened the lane earlier, tamping down the dust. As Noah guided Janey past the cottage and onto the part of the lane used mostly by his family, Rachel enjoyed the cooler evening temperature and most especially Noah's company.

They said little at first. Rachel thought that it might be because they felt comfortable and content in each other's company.

Noah pulled up on the leathers to stop the buggy. "Look!" He gestured toward animals in the field on the left.

Rachel beamed. "Deer! And so many."

There must have been five or six deer standing in the field. They ran and jumped across the lane far head of them and then disappeared through a windbreak of trees and out of sight.

Noah grinned at her as, under his guidance, Janey continued down the lane. "We may see raccoon or fox," he said.

Rachel narrowed her gaze as she searched the surrounding scenery for signs of animal life. Noah continued to drive for a time until they reached a stream where he parked the buggy and helped her to alight.

"I used to play here a lot as a child. I usually got in trouble for slipping and falling into the stream. *Mam* was never happy to see me arrive home drenched in water and mud." He smiled at the memory. "She wasn't angry—not really. She gave me a scolding, but I got the sense that she didn't really mind…as long as I wasn't hurt and got home safe."

"Your *mudder* is an amazing woman," Rachel said sincerely. She liked Katie Lapp. Katie had been kind to her from the first, understanding what had happened to her during and after her accident, mentioning it once to let her know she understood and then never mentioning it again. She had seemed to sense Rachel's need for privacy and the secret that Rachel kept from all but her family.

There was a large boulder half-submerged in the dirt; it made a good perch on which to sit and reflect as one listened to the gurgling stream.

Noah smiled as he gestured for her to sit. Rachel sat and he settled on the rock beside her.

She could smell his clean scent, hear the subtle inhale and exhale of his breath. His nearness made her heart sing.

They sat for a time in silence, disturbed only occasionally as a thought came to one or the other.

"Where does the stream go?" she asked.

Rachel had the strongest urge to take off her shoes and wade into the cool depths of the stream.

Noah bent and removed his shoes. Rachel didn't wait but a heartbeat before she untied her own shoelaces and rolled down her black stockings. In unison and without words, they reached out to clasp hands as they stepped into the stream and felt the cool water swirl about their bare ankles and the mud beneath their toes and the soles of their feet.

"Be careful of the rocks," Noah warned just as Rachel moved a step and felt a hard edge beneath the water. She gasped and started to tumble, but Noah grabbed her closer, steadying her. The feel of Noah's chest pressed close stole Rachel's breath and made her face heat.

He released her quickly but that one quick moment stayed in her memory, leaving an imprint.

"Are ya hurt?" he asked as he helped her out of the water.

"Nay," she said breathlessly. "I was startled, that's all." She managed a smile of thanks. "It would have been a long ride home if I'd gotten soaked to the skin."

Darkness had descended quickly. Rachel could barely see enough to put on her stockings. After he put on his shoes, Noah went to the buggy and pulled a flashlight out from under the seat, and switched it on so that Rachel could see. She put on her shoes, and with Noah's help, she scrambled to her feet.

"I'll take ya home," he said.

She nodded. "I enjoyed the outing."

"Ya did?" He walked to her side of the buggy and held out his hand.

She placed her hand in his. *"Ja."*

"Gut." Clasping her fingers, he helped her step up into the buggy. "You'll meet with me again?"

Rachel made herself comfortable as she took her seat. "I'll come again."

Noah was pleased as he circled the buggy to grab hold of Janey's lead, turning her back in the right direction, before he stopped to hop up onto the driver's side. It had been a wonderful night with the girl he was sure was God's choice for him. He just had to be patient and convince her that he would be the best husband for her.

A light breeze stirred the air, making the ride back pleasant. They were silent for a time until Rachel exclaimed with wonder, "Look, lightning bugs!"

She'd always loved them as a child and the sight of them still gave her enjoyment. There were tiny flashes of light in the wooded area not far from the lane. They looked a lot like the Christmas lights that the English had in their homes and businesses.

"They are nice to see," Noah agreed, and then the *hoo hoo ho-oot* of an owl once, and then again, drew his attention toward a treetop. He searched for the bird but couldn't see it. Still, he knew the call. "Great horned owl."

Rachel cocked her head to listen. The sound came again and she smiled. "Do you have any barn owls? We have them on the farm in Millersburg."

"We did. Haven't seen or heard from any in a long time."

The mare's hooves made a muffled clip-clop in the dirt. Rachel enjoyed the sound and Noah's company. Tomorrow school would start, and she would be busy with her students.

The wagon jerked. Old Janey whinnied and snorted as she balked at continuing.

"Walk on! Walk on!" Noah commanded, but he could sense that something was wrong. He aimed the flashlight along the woods line and caught the glint of two eyes and the outline of an animal.

Rachel froze with fear. *"Noah!"* she screamed.

Chapter Fifteen

"Coyote! Hold on, Rachel!" he said just as the coyote broke from the trees to run toward the buggy.

Rachel stifled a gasp of fright as old Janey went wild and half reared in the traces. Rachel held on tightly as Noah fought to control the plunging mare. The coyote stopped in the middle of the lane in front of them, stared at them a moment, then dashed away into the fields.

"Gently! Gently! Easy now, Janey," Noah crooned. "You all right, Rachel?"

"Holding on!" She was familiar with coyotes; they'd been a problem in Ohio, especially on a neighbor's farm. The sight of one filled her with terror, but that fear was nothing compared to the deep-seated panic that the buggy would overturn and she would be trapped in the tangle of wood and spinning wheels.

"*Gut!* Easy, girl. Easy." Noah held on to the leathers, soothing the horse with his voice. When Janey settled a bit, he jumped down from the wagon and moved carefully toward the animal's head, where he continued to speak softly to ease her fear.

Janey trembled and danced nervously, ears twitching and eyes rolling back to show the whites. Rachel clutched the edge of the wagon seat.

"*Gut* girl," Noah was telling the horse.

Slowly, Rachel's tension eased. "Is she all right?" Rachel asked. "And what about the coyote?"

"*Ja,* Janey is fine. She could sense the coyote before we saw it. Don't worry. The animal is long gone. I'll tell my *vadder* and brothers to keep an eye out for it, but I doubt we'll see it again. I think we frightened it as much as it scared Janey."

"May I have the flashlight?" Rachel asked as she climbed down from the wagon.

Noah handed it to her. She shined the light on the woods and across the field. There was no sign of an animal...neither a movement in the brush nor a glint of two strange eyes.

"We have coyotes in Ohio," she told him. "They ate a neighbor's chickens and then they went after his black Lab. The dog was killed."

Noah studied her face in the lamplight and saw how upset she was. It hadn't helped that the buggy had almost overturned. It must have reminded her of her first day in Lancaster County.

"I think he is long gone, Rachel," he said softly.

She shuddered. "I hope you're right."

Janey trembled and balked, still shaken by the coyote encounter. "We'd best walk her back," Noah said. "Can you make it?"

"It's not far. I'll be fine," Rachel said. She wasn't in a hurry to get back into a buggy being pulled by a spooked horse.

Noah held on to the bridle and with Rachel beside him started to walk back toward the schoolyard. "Rachel...you all right?"

"*Ja.* I am fine."

Noah paused to examine her features. What he saw reassured him. "Let's get you home, then." He rubbed the horse's neck. "You too, Janey."

The air was still; the song of insects filled the night. The darkness around them lit up here and there with the flash of fireflies. Rachel heard Noah's muffled footsteps mingled with the sound of hers and the dull rhythmic thuds of the mare's hooves on the dirt road. She chanced a look at Noah and saw the outline of his features in the outer glow of the flashlight he held. His brown eyes glistened in the light, his expression looked serious. Rachel had the strongest urge to grab his hand and hold on tightly, but she kept her head and continued to walk silently beside him.

After a fifteen-minute walk down the dirt road, Noah caught a glimpse of the teacher's cottage ahead. As they approached, he noted with a soft inner smile the flowers planted on each side of the front door. He had seen Rachel and her cousins digging in the dirt not long ago. They had done a nice job of arranging the petunias, marigolds and vinca plants.

"Home," Noah announced as they reached the cottage. "I'm sorry you had to walk back."

Rachel met his gaze. "I'm not." She appeared to hesitate, as if wanting to say something more, but was unable to find the right words. "I enjoyed the buggy ride."

"And the walk?"

She beamed at him. "*Ja.* The walk was the best part."

"I'll see you tomorrow?"

"*Schuul* starts tomorrow," Rachel told him.

He'd known about school, but he'd hoped she wouldn't use it as an excuse not to meet with him. "*Ja,* but it will end by three o'clock or so." Noah reached out, captured her hand. "You will think about what I said?"

"Noah…"

"It's all right, Rachel." He reached over to open the door. He peeked inside to make sure all was well. "*Gut* night," he said softly. He wouldn't push her, but he wondered if he'd kept his heart from showing in his eyes. "I will see you soon."

He saw her swallow.

"*Ja.*"

His smile was crooked. "Have a good first day of *schuul.*"

Rachel watched as Noah walked Janey and the buggy onto the road and continued to stand at the door until Noah disappeared from sight.

Early the next morning, Rachel stood at the door to the one-room Amish schoolhouse and smiled at her new students as they filtered inside. She nodded at each child who passed her, mentioning those she knew by name.

"John. Jacob. Mary Elizabeth." She smiled at several other children whose names she had yet to learn.

Within minutes, every child had taken a seat, and Rachel stood in the front of the classroom and introduced herself, speaking in the Amish German dialect.

The older children already received most of their education in English. This school year would be the first time for the youngest children to begin their English lessons, but time and their quick minds would soon have them chattering away like the others.

The day went well. The children seemed eager to be back in the classroom, except for one or two boys whose attention drifted until Rachel called it back.

At lunch break, the children opened their packed

lunches and ate at their desks before going outside to play. As they did during class, the older students helped the younger new students get adjusted. They showed them the swings in the schoolyard. While the younger children played on the swings, the older boys played catch with a baseball. Soon it was time for the afternoon lesson to commence. The littlest of her students practiced writing As and Bs while the older ones read from a reader designed to teach them about community life.

Rachel dismissed the class just after two-thirty in the afternoon. "I will see you tomorrow morning," she said with a smile. She had given them little homework on their first day of class. The children had enough to do to help out at home; they didn't need to be overworked by school.

After her students left, Rachel straightened the classroom before she exited the school and locked the door. She turned to head home and then gasped. Noah Lapp stood about three yards away, as if waiting for her.

"How was your first day as our Happiness teacher?" he asked conversationally, but she thought she detected a hint of anxiety beneath his pleasant demeanor.

"We had a *gut* day. The children were happy to be back in class." She paused. "Most of them were. My cousin John is still unconvinced he needs to come to school." Rachel studied him a moment as he accompanied her toward the cottage, sensing something odd in his mood. "Is something wrong?"

Noah attempted to smile. *"Nay."* He halted near her front steps and waited for her to unlock the door. "Rachel—"

She faced him. *"Ja?"* Today, he wore a short-sleeved maroon shirt with his triblend denim pants. It looked as if he had combed his hair recently before putting on his wide-brimmed straw hat.

He held her glance and then looked away toward the road, almost as if in a daze. After several seconds of silence, he finally said, "You had a nice time last night, *ja?*"

She nodded. "I did."

"I'm sorry if you were frightened." He seemed distressed about the coyote sighting and the unplanned walk back.

Rachel caught and held his gaze, her smile soft. "Noah, I would have been more frightened if you hadn't been there taking control."

He seemed pleased by her response. "The coyote—"

Rachel felt herself tense up. "*Ja,* I didn't like that part, but we had a nice time at the stream and before... and I didn't mind the walk. Really." She waited a heartbeat and then asked, "Did you find him?" She straightened her white *kapp,* pretending to be indifferent, that the idea of the coyote in the area didn't bother her.

"Ya don't need to worry about him any longer. He made the mistake of venturing onto an Englisher's farm and raiding his henhouse. The man took prompt care of him."

Rachel flinched. She didn't want the animal to hurt or bother anyone, but neither did she want to see it harmed. Noah was quiet for a time. She stood studying him, wondering what was on his mind.

He seemed reluctant to speak and what he said startled her. "Rachel, I know someone hurt you in the past, but I won't hurt you. You believe me?"

She felt her heart thumping. This wasn't a subject she was ready to discuss with him. Seeing how genuinely upset he seemed, she said softly, "I believe you won't hurt me." She touched his shoulder and then pulled back as if burned. "Sometimes things happen that cause someone to be hurt."

"I will wait for you, Rachel Hostetler," he said, his expression earnest. "I will wait until you trust me enough to believe in me…until you'll say yes to our courting." He left, heading toward the main road.

"Noah—" she called out, unable to help herself.

He stopped and faced her.

"I will see you tonight?" she asked. She no longer cared if he knew that she wanted to spend time with him.

"It is my brother's birthday," Noah said quietly. "Will you come to the house?"

"I don't know—"

"Come," he urged. "My mother will be glad to see you. The Kings are coming, too."

Her aunt and uncle would be there? That fact gave Rachel comfort. No one would think anything of her presence if her relatives were there.

"I'll come," she said.

"I'll stay and wait for you then. *Mam* is making Joseph's favorite."

Rachel entered the house. "Come in, then, while I put away a few things. So it's young Joseph's birthday."

Noah seemed larger than life as he followed her into her kitchen. "*Ja,* the youngest Lapp child before Hannah."

Rachel set her lunch bag on the counter, and then she opened a cabinet and took down two glasses. "Iced tea?"

"That would be nice." He sat at her kitchen table and Rachel poured him a glass and set it before him. She put out a plate of cookies and he grinned as he grabbed one and took a bite.

"I will be back in a few minutes," Rachel said as Noah enjoyed a chocolate-chip cookie and drank his tea. He waved at her as he helped himself to a chocolate cookie iced with chocolate frosting.

Rachel headed to her room and took off her school apron, replacing it with a clean one. She'd worn her spring-green dress for the first day of school. She splashed water on her face before she returned to the kitchen to find Noah staring out the window, apparently deep in thought.

"Noah."

He jumped as if startled and rose to his feet. "Ready?"

"Do you think Joseph will like some of these cookies?" she asked.

Noah smiled. "*Ja,* he will, and if not, his big brother does."

Rachel laughed. She checked to see that the back kitchen door was locked before she and Noah left the house by the front door.

"I thought we could walk," Noah said when he saw her look for his buggy.

"It is a nice day for a walk," Rachel agreed as she fell into step beside him. They went through the schoolyard and then cut across the field until they reached the dirt driveway that led to the Lapp home.

As they followed the lane toward the house, they heard the wheels of a buggy and the clip-clop of the horse that pulled it.

"Noah! Rachel!" It was the King carriage. "Want a ride?"

Noah shook his head. "We're almost there. Mae, Amos. Glad you could come by this evening. Charlotte, Nancy." He nodded at each one in turn. "Is that John and Joshua I see hiding in the back of the buggy?"

Rachel could hear Joshua's giggle before she saw him peek up alongside his older brother. "John," she said. "Any trouble with homework?"

"*Nay.* Not much to do. It didn't take me long."

"I thought I'd go easy on the first day. Be prepared!" She saw John's eyes widen, and she laughed to let him know she was teasing him.

She spent a pleasant evening at the Lapp residence. It was wonderful to see Katie again. Rachel genuinely cared for the woman, and Katie seemed to know how much she enjoyed holding Hannah, for it wasn't long before the baby was asleep in the young woman's arms.

The evening was pleasant, not cool but not too warm. After supper, they sat on the front porch, and even the men joined them. Soon, the time came for her to go home. She had another day of class the next morning, and she needed a good night's sleep.

Noah volunteered to escort her home. He matched her steps as they strolled down the lane and then entered the field. Rachel appreciated that she felt easy and lighthearted whenever she was in Noah's presence.

Noah noticed that Rachel seemed to enjoy the evening and that she wasn't in the least afraid as he walked her home. If she thought of the coyote, she didn't mention it.

"Everything all right at *schuul?*" he asked. "Any problems with the construction?"

"*Nay,* the construction is fine and all went well." Rachel felt his presence like a warm blanket of protection. She'd never felt this way about anyone. He made her feel safe, cared for…special.

She stepped inside, and he hesitated in the door opening. "Rachel…"

She turned to him and said, "*Ja*. Noah—"

Noah looked confused…and then as he studied her face, he felt warmth radiating inside his chest. *"Ja?"* He waited hopefully.

"You may court me." She stared at him. "If you want to—"

"If I want—" Noah whooped for joy as he lifted her within his strong arms and spun her around before setting her down again. "Rachel, I—"

Rachel had laughed as he'd spun her. "I know," she said. "Me, too."

He grinned as he caught and held her hand. "We can go for a ride tomorrow. John can chaperone us. We can—" He suddenly frowned. "I'll need to talk with someone about us, but who?"

Rachel shrugged. "My parents are in Ohio. My only relatives here are Aunt Mae and Uncle Amos, and they love you. Talk with Uncle Amos. I don't think there will be a problem." Eyes softening, Noah continued to study her. Rachel loved the giddy way he made her feel. "I hate to say this, but it's late, and I have a class to teach tomorrow morning."

"*Ja*. I will go," Noah said, "but Rachel?"

She tilted her head as she gazed up at him. "Is something wrong?"

"*Nay*. I only wanted to tell ya that you've made me a happy man tonight."

The look in his eyes made her feel dizzy with joy. Rachel gazed at him with tenderness. She dared to lift a hand and caress his cheek. "And you've made me a happy woman, Noah Lapp. Now, you'd best get home before your *mam* and *dat* wonder what happened to you."

He spun to leave and turned back to flash her a warm smile. "*Gut* night, Rachel. Pleasant dreams."

"*Gut* night, Noah. I had a nice time tonight."

"Me, too," he said, and then he left, but not before glancing back several times to see if she was still at the door watching him, and she was.

The weeks that followed were filled with wonder and happiness for Rachel. She taught school with the enjoyment of one who loves to teach. Noah came by the school often for one reason or another. It was the Friday after her dinner with the Lapps that she and Noah were seen out and about in the wagon together with only Rachel's cousin John King as chaperone. Rachel was surprised when Noah first came with the large wagon instead of the courting buggy, but considering what had happened the last three times she'd ridden in one, she was secretly glad. Still, did folks realize that she and Noah were courting? If they didn't at first, they would soon. Noah and she were seen often in each other's company, always accompanied by one cousin or another— mostly John and occasionally little Joshua.

Aunt Mae and Uncle Amos couldn't be happier. If they were surprised by Noah's interest in Rachel, they didn't show it.

"You're a *gut* girl, Rachel. We are happy you have taken a liking to Noah," Aunt Mae said. "Noah is a *gut* boy."

"He is a *gut man,* Mae," her husband corrected softly.

"*Ja,* this is so," Aunt Mae said, "but it seems only yesterday when he and our girls were small children."

Rachel wondered how her aunt and uncle felt about

her relationship with Noah after it became obvious to the community that Noah had chosen Rachel over Charlotte. It was during the second week of her and Noah walking out together that Rachel learned that several women had approached Charlotte to commiserate with her the loss of Noah's affections. Charlotte had reacted with laughter at the notion and expressed to all her genuine happiness at her cousin's good fortune to have Noah court her.

"Abram and I have been seeing each other secretly," Charlotte had confided to Rachel. "Abram is shy, but he seems to enjoy spending time with me." Charlotte told Rachel that she had high hopes that their budding friendship would lead into something special and long lasting.

It was an early Saturday morning when Charlotte came to visit Rachel at the cottage. She knocked and Rachel was pleasantly surprised to see her and invited her in for breakfast.

"You haven't eaten?" Rachel said.

"*Nay,* I wouldn't mind a bite."

"I can make you eggs and I have coffee cake."

"Coffee cake will be fine," Charlotte said, taking a seat at Rachel's kitchen table. "And tea, please."

Rachel felt her cousin studying her as she poured a cup of tea and cut Charlotte a piece of cake. She looked up and met her gaze. "What?"

"It becomes you," Charlotte said with a little half smile. When Rachel looked confused, Charlotte continued, "Courting. Or should I say, Noah becomes you."

Rachel blushed as she sat down. "He is wonderful."

"I told you so," Charlotte said, sounding satisfied.

"And I thought you were saying so because you were in love with him yourself."

"What?" Charlotte looked stunned. She thought a moment and then began to chuckle. "I never thought… I guess you might have seen it that way. I wanted you to know how amazing he is so that you'd see him for what he is—the man for you."

"I can see that now…" Rachel sipped and swallowed some tea. "Sometimes I feel so happy that it scares me." She hesitated and then admitted, "You know what happened with Abraham Beiler."

Charlotte shook her head. *"Nay,* not really. I know you and he were in a buggy accident…"

"We were courting, Charlotte. I got hurt and spent some time in the hospital," Rachel said lightly, unwilling to go into detail about the horror of that time. "That was the last day of our courtship."

"Oh, Rachel…"

"Noah is different," Rachel said. "He makes me feel special…and loved."

Charlotte smiled. *"Gut,* because he loves you."

Rachel felt a jolt to hear her cousin say it. Noah and she hadn't reached the point of such discussion. They were enjoying their courtship, but the depth of their feelings had yet to be stated.

"You couldn't do better than Noah, Rachel." Charlotte sipped her tea.

"And I hope all works out well with Abram."

"I think it will," Charlotte said as she put down her cup. "Abram is coming to the house this afternoon. He says he wants a word with *Dat.*" She lowered her voice. "I hope it's for the reason I want it to be."

Rachel got up and went over to hug Charlotte. "It will be. I can feel it in my heart that today will be special for you."

They ate their coffee cake and drank their tea. Soon,

Charlotte got up to leave. "Tell me all about it tomorrow," Rachel said.

"You won't come to dinner?"

"*Nay.* Noah is coming to take me to his house. Katie is making something special, he says."

The cousins hugged and wished each other a fine day, and then Rachel set to work cleaning the cottage and baking something delicious to take to the Lapp table this evening.

Katie Lapp was glad to see her. Rachel beamed at the woman as Katie accepted her cherry-chocolate pie and then led her into the kitchen, where she invited Rachel to sit down.

"I'd like to help," Rachel said.

"No, please. You sit and relax. You work hard enough as it is. If you like, you can hold Hannah." Katie left a moment and came back with her daughter in her arms.

Rachel gladly accepted the little girl and set her on her lap. She played with the child's fingers to entertain her.

"You've made my son happy," Katie said as she set down a cup of tea before Rachel, who nodded her thanks.

"I've never met anyone like Noah," Rachel said. "He is kind and generous." She paused a moment. "You raised a *gut* son." She was having fun with Noah. She didn't want to think about it ending. She didn't want to believe that there was a chance that she couldn't have children. The possibility that a child wasn't in her future could ruin her relationship with Noah. Maybe she could make an appointment with a doctor to see if it was true....

It wasn't long before dinner was ready and Rachel

helped Katie put out the meal. Katie, Hannah and Rachel were the only females at the table filled with eight men, including little Joseph. It was clear to Rachel that the Lapp males liked to eat and enjoyed Katie's cooking. Tomorrow was Sunday. There were other food items already prepared for the next day when there would be no work, including cooking, except for the simplest chores that couldn't be avoided, like caring for the animals.

"We'll be visiting the Kings tomorrow," Katie said. "Rachel, you'll be there as well?"

"*Ja.* I miss my aunt and uncle. It will be *gut* to spend the day with them."

Not long after the meal, Noah took Rachel home. He halted at the door, reluctant to leave her. "My family loves you."

"I love them, too."

He flashed her a grin. "And me?"

Rachel's heart skipped a beat. "We wouldn't be courting if I didn't like you."

"Only like?"

She sighed. "Noah…"

He held up his hand and stepped back a few paces. He gazed at her with affection. "I will see you tomorrow."

"See you tomorrow," she echoed.

Noah stepped up to her quickly, took hold of her hands. "Think of me tonight," he said as he gave her fingers a gentle squeeze. Then he released her and was gone.

Chapter Sixteen

The following Wednesday, Rachel dismissed her students and then straightened the classroom as usual. She didn't expect Noah to stop by, for he had errands to run for his father, so she lingered, planning her lesson for the next day and erasing the chalkboard in the front of the room.

The pain, when it hit her, was sharp and made her cry out and clutch her abdomen. She gasped and moved to her desk chair, taking a moment to sit down. She took several calming breaths and the pain subsided for a few seconds before coming back full force.

Dear Lord, she prayed, *don't let this be my injury from the accident!*

When she'd gotten hurt in the buggy accident with Abraham, she had been told that her injuries were serious...that they might come back to trouble her in the future.

Tears filled her eyes as she hugged her abdomen. *What if this pain is the result of the old injury?*

She stood and felt nauseous, the pain was so great.

How was she to get help? She couldn't walk anywhere. She pressed lightly on her abdomen and inhaled sharply.

"What am I going to do? Please, Lord, help me." Then she heard a voice and thought she'd imagined it.

"Rachel!" Charlotte called excitedly. "Rachel, I've got something to tell you!" Her cousin entered the schoolhouse and froze as she saw Rachel. "Rachel!" She hurried to her side. "What's wrong?"

"Terrible pain in my belly. Hurts bad." Rachel tried to rise and then gasped and clutched her midsection. "Can you take me to the doctor?"

"Noah," Charlotte said, "I should get Noah."

"Nay! Please don't worry him. You can tell him after I find out what's wrong."

"I don't know," Charlotte hedged. "He'll want to help."

"Nay! Please, Charlotte, promise me. I don't want to upset him." She didn't want him to learn about her injuries in this way. She had tried to put what the doctors had said out of her mind, but now she was getting a painful reminder.

"I promise." Charlotte helped Rachel to her feet. "Good thing I brought the buggy. But I'm not taking you to the doctor. You need a hospital."

Hospital. Rachel closed her eyes tightly. She had spent more time than she'd ever wanted in a hospital, but she knew her cousin was right. "How far is it?"

"I'm not sure. It must be four miles or more." Charlotte studied her with concern. "How about *Dat?* Can I get him?"

"Nay." Rachel opened her eyes and swayed. "Just take me, please." Tears slipped from beneath her lowered lids.

Charlotte helped Rachel into the buggy and then ran

around the back of the vehicle to hop into the other side. "How is the pain?"

"It's eased for a minute, but—" Rachel grimaced as the pain returned.

Charlotte clicked her tongue and guided the buggy onto the road in the direction of the local hospital near Lancaster. "We should stop and tell *Mam.*"

"*Please,* Charlotte." She didn't want everyone to know. She'd had to suffer the physical pain and the emotional hurt of knowing that the past buggy accident might have caused enough injury to cause her current pain and possible barrenness.

She loved Noah. She didn't want to lose him. She shouldn't have agreed to their courtship, but she wanted to be with him, and she had begun to believe the doctors had been wrong. Besides, they hadn't actually said that she couldn't have children. Only that it might be difficult for her to conceive and give birth.

The ride toward the hospital seemed to take forever. Rachel sat with her eyes closed, hunched over and praying through the pain. Soon, she felt the buggy shift and turn right. Rachel opened her eyes and saw the Peachy farm.

Her cousin faced her. "I'm getting Abram to help us."

"Charlotte—"

"You're feeling worse, Rachel. I'd feel better if Abram drove you to the hospital."

A sharp pain made Rachel gasp and cry out. She wasn't in any condition to object.

Charlotte pulled the buggy into Abram's yard and then ran toward the house. "Abram! Abram!"

Within seconds, Rachel heard quick footsteps as someone approached. The buggy dipped as he climbed in. But it wasn't Abram Peachy, as expected; it was

Noah. Rachel looked at him and tried to smile but tears filled her eyes as the pain ripped through her abdomen. Despite her words to Charlotte earlier, she was glad to see him.

"I'm taking you to the hospital," he said, and she jerked her head in a nod.

Abram and Charlotte came out of the house, hurrying toward the vehicle.

"I'm going to take her!" Noah called out. "No time to waste!"

"Go, Noah! Abram will take me home. *Mam* will want to know." Charlotte shot Abram a glance.

"*Ja.* I will take her home. Go!" Abram put a comforting arm around Charlotte's shoulders.

Noah guided the buggy around, and then with a loud *yah,* he flicked the leathers to spur the horse-drawn vehicle down the lane and onto the main road.

Flashing her a quick glance, Noah felt an awful burning in the pit of his stomach at the sight of Rachel's tears. She was in terrible pain, and he felt helpless. *Dear Lord, please help me get her to the hospital safely.*

Rachel sobbed quietly. She held her belly, her gaze focused on the road ahead. She looked pale and very ill.

"Noah," she finally said, "I'm going to be sick."

He pulled back on the leathers, and after the horse slowed, he guided the buggy to the side of the road, where he jumped down and raced around the vehicle to help Rachel. She made it only two steps before she vomited. Concerned, Noah eyed the buggy, thought about their distance to the hospital, and the realization terrified him.

Rachel was too sick to feel more than only slightly embarrassed. The cramping had made her nauseous and the ride in the racing buggy hadn't helped.

When she was done, she turned to find Noah flagging down a car.

"Please," he told the driver who finally stopped to help. It was the Englisher who had helped to put out Abram's barn fire. "Rachel is ill. We need to get to the hospital. Can you take us?"

"Of course," Tom Drulis said. "Get in." The gray-haired man had a kind face. He gestured toward a nearby house. "Can you move the buggy over there? I know the Beckers. I'll tell them someone will come back for it later."

Noah was grateful, and after seeing Rachel safely into the backseat of the car, he quickly moved the buggy to a hitching post in the Beckers' barnyard. Kyle Becker came out of the house, and Tom spoke with him. The farmer assured Noah that he would water and take good care of the horse.

Soon, Noah joined Rachel in the backseat of Tom Drulis's car, speeding toward the hospital. Noah put his arm around Rachel and held her as she cried through her pain. They arrived in less than ten minutes. It would have taken Noah a good half hour or more to reach the hospital in the buggy, and the Kings' horse would have suffered.

Noah thanked Tom Drulis profusely as he helped Rachel out of the man's car. Tom promised to return later to see if he could help.

As they entered the building, Noah noted the hospital's strange medicinal smell. He eased Rachel carefully into a chair and then hurried to speak with the triage nurse.

"See the girl there?" Noah said anxiously. "Her name is Rachel Hostetler. She has had sharp pains in her lower belly for some time. She got sick on the way over. I think there is something terribly wrong!"

The nurse looked up with a bored expression until she met Noah's gaze. She frowned and then glanced toward Rachel. Rachel sat in the chair, hunched over, sobbing. Noah saw the quick change on the woman's face as she came out from behind her desk and approached. She gently asked Rachel about the pain. She helped Rachel over to the triage area and took her vitals. Noah followed closely. "She has a fever," the woman said with a frown. "Someone is coming to take her back now."

Rachel barely heard what was being said, she hurt so much. She thought someone said something about being taken back, and then she thought that the woman asked Noah to wait outside in the waiting room.

"Nay!" Rachel said. "Can't he come with me? Just for a little while?"

"Until the doctor comes in to examine you," the nurse said.

They moved Rachel into a curtained area in the emergency room. Noah was barely there two minutes when he was asked to leave.

Holding her gaze, Noah clasped her hand and gave her a reassuring squeeze. "I'll be here when you need me," he said before he left as ordered.

The doctor who came in to see Rachel was a woman. Dr. Moss introduced herself and asked if she could examine Rachel. Rachel lay back on the examining table, and when Dr. Moss pressed on her abdomen, she flinched and then cried out as the woman probed a specific area.

"Any nausea or vomiting?" she asked Rachel.

"Ja," Rachel whispered miserably. She told Dr. Moss about getting sick and then about the buggy accident

and severe abdominal injury she'd suffered. "They said I might have trouble with it again."

Dr. Moss frowned. "I'd like to run some tests, including a blood draw. You're running a fever. I think I know what's wrong, but I want to make sure before we proceed."

Rachel felt her throat tighten as her tears overflowed. She knew what the doctor was going to tell her—that the internal injury she'd suffered had become infected. *Please, Lord, help me to be strong.*

Noah was pacing the waiting area when Abram, Charlotte, Mae and Amos arrived. Tom Drulis had stopped by the Kings' to inform the family and had offered to drive them into town. Upon seeing Noah, Mae rushed over.

"How is she?" she asked. Noah saw Mae's concern.

"She's still inside. The doctor hasn't come out yet." He felt sick with worry. Rachel meant so much to him; he didn't want anything to happen to her. He hated seeing her in pain.

It seemed like a long wait before the doctor came out with news.

"How is Rachel?" Noah asked anxiously.

"Rachel is going to need emergency surgery," Dr. Moss said. "She has acute appendicitis and they are prepping her for the O.R. now."

"Will she be all right?" Mae asked.

"As long as we get to the appendix before it ruptures. She's in a lot of pain, so we need to get her to the OR now."

Noah rubbed his forehead beneath the brim of his hat. "May I see her?"

Dr. Moss looked to Mae. "You are her relative, and there is only time for one quick visit."

"It's fine. Let Noah see her. She'll want to see him." Mae turned toward Noah. "Tell her that we'll be here for whatever she needs."

"I will." Noah met Mae's gaze. "I appreciate this. I know how worried you are about her."

"Go, Noah. Cheer her up."

"If you want to see her, you must go quickly," Dr. Moss said.

Noah was taken into the emergency room, to the curtained area where Rachel lay. She wore a hospital gown and was covered modestly with a blanket. She still wore her *kapp;* the rest of her clothing had been put elsewhere for safekeeping.

"Rachel," he whispered as he hurried to her side. "I'm sorry." She looked pale and vulnerable. She was hooked up to an IV and a machine monitored her heartbeat. He felt helpless that he couldn't do more for her.

Rachel managed a small smile. "Why are ya sorry, Noah? It's not your fault that I have appendicitis. You got me here quickly."

As she spoke, medical workers came to take her to the operating room.

"Your aunt Mae and Charlotte are outside. Aunt Mae wanted me to tell you that they will be here for whatever you need." He gently took hold of her hand. "I'll be here for you, Rachel. Always."

"You're a *gut* man, Noah Lapp," Rachel said and then she grimaced and closed her eyes, clearly in pain.

"Time to go," the nurse said.

She opened her eyes and met Noah's gaze. "I'll be all right," she said, and then she was taken from the area and Noah was led outside, back into the waiting room.

The Lapps arrived, all seven of Noah's siblings along with his *mam* and *dat.* Carrying her daughter, Hannah, Katie rushed up to her son. "How is Rachel?"

"She has appendicitis," Noah said.

"Mae told me, but *how is she?*"

Noah's mouth curved slightly upward. "She says she will be fine. She is in a lot of pain. I wish I could do something to help her."

"You already did," Mae said, joining the two of them. "You had the good sense to have someone drive her in a car and God blessed us in that it belonged to Tom Drulis." Mae touched his cheek. "Take heart, Noah. I have faith that Rachel will be well soon."

Noah nodded, but then bowed his head and said a silent prayer. After a time, other members of their church community filled the waiting room, coming in support of Rachel, Noah and the Kings. A hospital worker entered the room and told them they couldn't stay. "There isn't enough room for all of you," the woman said.

The Zooks, the Masts and the Hershbergers took their leave, asking Mae to keep them informed about Rachel's recovery.

"See that she rests," Alta Hershberger instructed Mae.

Noah saw Mae control a small smile. "I will," Mae assured her.

After a few moments of silent prayer, most of the church community members left. Only Mae, Charlotte, Noah, Katie and baby Hannah remained.

Two hours later, the emergency-clinic door opened and Dr. Moss came out, still in surgical scrubs. "Rachel did well," she told them. "If we'd been much longer, the appendix would have ruptured. She will be sore when she wakes up, but fine."

"May we see her?" Noah asked, anxious to be with her again. He needed to see for himself that she was better.

"I'm afraid not," the doctor said. "She's in the recovery room. We don't expect her to be ready for visitors until tomorrow morning. She's likely to sleep the rest of the afternoon and night." She glanced about the waiting room, and seemed to take note of those who had stayed for news of Rachel. "You should go home and get some rest. Rachel won't even know you have gone. You'll be able to see her first thing tomorrow. Is there some way I can reach you if needed?"

"Whittier's Store near us has a telephone," Noah said. "They often take messages for us." He waited while the doctor retrieved pen and paper from a worker's desk before he gave her the number. "Mention my name, and Mr. Whittier will make sure I get the message."

Dr. Moss jotted down the information. "Go home," she urged again. "You can see Rachel in the morning."

After the doctor left, Noah sat down. "I don't think I should leave her."

"Noah," Katie said softly. She gently touched her son's cheek. "You've been through a lot. Rachel will want to see you tomorrow. You should rest today so that you are at your best for her in the morning."

Noah met his mother's loving gaze and felt overwhelmed by the events of the day. He *was* exhausted… tired, worried and frightened for the woman he loved. What *Mam* said made sense. He needed a good night's sleep.

He stood. "I'll go home…for Rachel. I need to fetch Amos's buggy. I left it at a neighbor of Tom Drulis's when Tom drove us here."

"Amos has our buggy. Yours is outside," Mae said.

"Tom picked up Jedidiah, who drove ours the rest of the way to the hospital. Your brother rode home with the Zooks, leaving us the buggy. Samuel brought your family buggy and then he and your other brothers got a ride home with the Hershbergers and Masts."

Noah approached Mae. "You will come with us?"

The woman smiled. "*Nay.* Amos is not far; Tom went back for him and our youngest. Amos took Joshua for an ice cream. He'll be back to take us home."

Shortly afterward, Noah, his mother and his sister climbed into the family buggy and headed home. Noah was quiet during the journey. Suddenly, he needed his mother to know how he felt. "*Mam,* I love her."

"I know you do." Katie shifted her daughter more comfortably in her arms.

"Someone hurt her in the past. I don't know who."

"*Ja.*" *Mam* looked as if she would say something more, but kept silent.

"I want to marry her. I'll wait until she agrees. I will be patient." He exhaled sharply. "She is worth the wait."

His mother's answer was to place a hand on his arm and give it a quick, light squeeze.

They were silent for a time. Hannah had fallen asleep on Katie's lap. The only sounds were the horse's hooves on macadam and the squeak of the buggy wheels as they turned over pavement.

"Noah, I have something I need you to do," Katie said after a time. "There is a pile of *The Budget* in the barn. I'd like you to gather the newspapers and bring them into the house. I would like your help sorting through them."

Rachel was in the hospital, and *Mam* was thinking about cleaning out the barn? He shrugged. "All right."

"Noah."

"Ja, Mam?" He turned toward her.

"Rachel will be fine."

He managed a smile. "I pray to the *gut* Lord that it is so."

Katie nodded. "It is always the best thing to do."

Chapter Seventeen

Early the next morning, Noah helped his mother into the buggy and then ran around to hop into the seat beside her. "Do ya think she'll be awake when we get there?" he asked.

Katie shifted to make herself comfortable and waved through the window to her eldest son, who would be in charge of the children until their return. "She may... especially if she slept all of yesterday afternoon and last night."

Noah flicked the leathers to spur the horse on. Today they were taking their horse Jerry John; he was eager to make better time with the young gelding.

"You never told me about Rachel's accident," he said.

"It wasn't my secret to tell." Katie straightened her *kapp* as she glanced at her son. "With all that's happened, I thought a little information might be helpful to you."

Noah couldn't control a grin. "And by having me 'help' sort through the newspapers..."

Katie nodded. "You just might stumble onto the issue with news from Millersburg...about a young woman involved in a courting-buggy accident." Her small smile faded as Rachel's misfortune that day seemed to have taken hold of her thoughts. "You went to see Mae?"

"*Ja*. She told me what happened. How Abraham Beiler left her while she was still recovering in the hospital." Noah scowled. "What type of man does that to a woman?"

"A guilt-ridden one, I'd say." Katie waved to a neighbor along the road. "Don't judge him too harshly, Noah. It wouldn't surprise me if he left because he couldn't face her."

"But to marry her best friend within months?" Noah shook his head. "I will try hard to think kindly of him." He brightened. "If not for his actions, then Rachel wouldn't have come to us, and I would not have met the woman I love."

His mother smiled at him and then turned to look out the side buggy window. She was silent for a time. Suddenly, she turned to him, placed a hand on his arm. "You know she suffered injuries in the accident," she said softly.

He patted her hand. "I know. Mae explained, but it makes not a bit of difference about how I feel about her. Knowing the truth, I love her even more."

Katie looked satisfied. "She loves you, but she is afraid of getting hurt again."

Noah knew how vulnerable Rachel was and there was no way he would ever hurt her. "I know. I will wait until she is ready…until I can prove to her that she has nothing to fear in our future together."

He could sense his mother's surprise. "You asked the Kings' permission."

"*Ja*. I wanted to do this right. They know that I will

not rush her. They are happy that we have found each other."

"As your *dat* and I are," Katie commented with a grin.

The ride, which Noah expected to last forever considering how eager he was to see Rachel, was over much more quickly than he thought it would be. He pulled into the hospital parking lot and around to the hitching post in the back of the building. He secured Jerry John and then helped his mother alight.

Katie smiled at him as he helped her step down. "You will make a fine husband."

Noah blinked. "Are you looking to have grandchildren?"

"I have a babe of my own still. Grandchildren, if and when they come, are blessings from God. I was not referring to that part of marriage."

Noah felt his stomach tighten as the truth of Rachel's pain hit him. "I know."

He reached into the buggy and withdrew a bouquet of wildflowers. He remembered how pleased she'd looked the first time he'd given her flowers. He hoped the posies would cheer her.

Katie looked at her son's face and the flowers he held carefully in his hands. "We should check on Rachel. I think she will be looking to have visitors now."

The pain in Rachel's abdomen wasn't as bad as it had been last night. She had awakened in the middle of the night, crying out, disturbed by the hospital surroundings. She had thought it was a year ago again, and the pain was from the buggy accident. She had sobbed as all the terror and heartache had come rushing in.

Upon hearing Rachel's cry, the night nurse had come

into the room and calmed her, explaining that she'd had an appendectomy. The woman had given Rachel something for the pain, and finally Rachel had been able to go back to sleep, sore but with the pain manageable and the terror of the past eased.

This morning another nurse had come and adjusted Rachel's bed so that she was more comfortable. Rachel had dozed on and off for a time until just a short while ago, when the pain had disturbed her sleep. She wondered where everyone had gone—Noah, Charlotte, Aunt Mae and Uncle Amos.

A hospital worker came into her room. The bed beside hers was empty; the woman who'd had gall-bladder surgery had been discharged the previous afternoon, the nurse had told her. Someone else would no doubt be moved into the room today.

"Would you like some Jell-O?" the girl asked. She had blond hair, not unlike Charlotte's, and she looked about sixteen in her pink uniform. Her name badge read "Jessie."

Rachel shook her head.

"I'm sorry," Jessie said, "but it's all you can have. You can have that or a cup of tea. You're on a liquid diet today."

Rachel managed a smile. "Thank you," she said easily in English, "but I don't need anything right now."

Jessie nodded as if she understood. "I'll come back later. Perhaps you'll want a cup of tea then."

"Thank you," Rachel said. She closed her eyes briefly and brought up the image of Noah's face. He had been so comforting and caring during the ride to, and at, the hospital. Where was he?

She felt a burning in her stomach. Abraham Beiler

had never come to see her. *But Noah is different, and he will come.*

She heard a familiar voice outside her room and thought, *Noah!* She opened her eyes as Noah and Katie Lapp stepped through the doorway.

"Rachel!" Noah hurried to her side.

"Noah!" she breathed. He was here, and she had never been so happy to see anyone.

"How are you feeling?"

She gave a crooked smile. "Sore, but much better... because of you."

"Rachel." Katie Lapp stepped forward. Rachel regarded the woman with warmth. "Katie. I'm so glad you came to see me." She gestured toward the chairs by the bed. Noah took the one closest to her head. Katie sat in the chair beside him.

"We were all worried about you," Katie said. "The waiting room was full—we were told that we couldn't all stay."

Tears glistened in Rachel's eyes. "Everyone came. That is wonderful to hear." She was moved by the concern of her new church community. "Please tell everyone how much I appreciate their concern." Noah handed her a bouquet of wildflowers. "These are beautiful, Noah." Smiling, she set them in her plastic water cup. Noah helped to hold the cup still for her.

"The Kings will be here later," Noah said. He reached out to grab hold of her hand. "*Mam* and I wanted to come first thing. Jedidiah is in charge of the children today."

Amused at the thought, Rachel raised her eyebrows. "I bet he isn't happy about that."

Katie smiled and regarded her with twinkling eyes. "It isn't the first time one of my sons has helped out.

With seven sons and a baby daughter, it is often necessary for one of them to lend a hand in the kitchen or garden."

"Did you see the doctor this morning?" Noah asked. He still held her hand, and Rachel enjoyed the contact.

Rachel flashed Katie a quick glance before returning her attention to Noah. "She was in earlier. I am doing as well as expected."

If it bothered Katie to see her son's open display of affection, Katie didn't show it. "You will stay at the Kings' during your recovery?"

Rachel frowned. "I had hoped to stay in the cottage."

Katie gave a nod. "We thought as much. We will take turns staying with you until you are well enough to be on your own."

"I didn't expect that—"

"Rachel," Noah interrupted softly, "it will be for your own good, and you know the women will enjoy it."

Rachel recalled the fun she'd had when her cousins had stayed with her the first few nights after she'd moved in. *"Ja,"* she said. "I know my cousins will."

The three of them talked for a time until an hour flew by. Katie rose. "I think I will go downstairs for some tea. Would you like some?"

Rachel shook her head. She thought she saw Katie and Noah exchange quick glances, but she might have been mistaken. "I'll have a chocolate milk shake," Noah said, and Rachel laughed.

"Of course it would be chocolate," she said.

Katie left and Rachel was alone with Noah. Noah stroked her hand and regarded her with a solemn expression. He seemed anxious, and Rachel frowned. "Noah, are ya all right?"

He seemed to pull himself up, and then his smile

for her held genuine warmth. "I am well, Rachel, but I was so afraid for you. Terrified that I would lose you."

"And as you can see I am fine. The doctor said the surgery went well."

"The Lord was watching over you. I'm relieved the doctor could operate before your appendix ruptured." He released her hand and stood for a moment. He gazed down at her. "Rachel, it is you that worries me. Charlotte said that you didn't want me to know…about how sick you were."

Rachel looked away briefly. "That was true—at first. But when you came, I felt glad. I knew you would take *gut* care of me…get me to the hospital quickly." She grabbed hold of his hand so that her fingers surrounded and squeezed his gently. "I didn't want you to worry." And she'd wanted to know for certain exactly what was wrong before letting him know. A crazy notion, she realized.

His expression softened as Noah sat and regarded her with warmth. "I'm glad to hear you say that." He moved to the edge of the chair, took hold of both her hands. "Rachel Hostetler, I want to marry you. Please marry me so that we can be together forever."

Stunned, heart beating wildly, Rachel could only stare at him. She loved Noah with all of her heart, but how could she say yes? How could she marry him if she couldn't give him a family?

"Noah, I love you, but I don't think I should marry you." She didn't see the hurt she'd expected; the only thing she saw was his fierce determination.

"Why not? You say you love me."

"There are things about me you don't know."

"You are already married?" he said jokingly, but the words fell flat.

Rachel shook her head. This was no joking matter, and she realized then that despite his expression, Noah was hurting. She knew she had to tell him everything. She knew it would cause him pain once he realized the reason they couldn't marry…but still, she had to tell him.

She blinked against tears. "A year ago this past winter, I was in a buggy accident, and I got seriously hurt. I spent weeks in the hospital."

She studied his face but couldn't read his expression. She hesitated until he nodded for her to go on. "It was a courting buggy…"

As if sensing her pain, Noah stroked her hands reassuringly. Her skin tingled under his touch.

"Noah, I was seriously injured…*here.*" She pulled a hand away to place it on the covers over her abdomen. She bit her lower lip and tears spilled from her eyes.

Noah hated seeing her tears. He could feel her pain as if it were his.

"You recovered," Noah said, "and you will do so again."

"Noah, I may not be able to have children," she said quickly. "You are so good with them; it wouldn't be fair to you…"

He smiled. "That's it? You can't marry me because it's possible you can't have a child?"

Rachel was stunned by his reaction. Noah looked almost relieved. But relieved by what?

"Rachel," he said. "I love you with all of my heart. I truly believe that the Lord wants us to be together. It doesn't matter if you can't have a child. I love *you.*"

"But children—you will make a good father."

"Then we will adopt. There are children who need

homes. Together, with our love, we can provide a *gut* home."

"Noah…"

Noah could tell that Rachel was afraid to believe that the solution was this simple. He knew that with Rachel by his side, he could live life as God intended…he could happily meet life's challenges head-on.

"I know all about the accident, Rachel," he admitted, "and Abraham Beiler. I am sorry you had to suffer through that. I am not sorry that Abraham Beiler was a fool, for if he hadn't been, then you and I wouldn't have met." He leaned forward, even closer to the bed. He recognized when she felt a tiny seedling of hope.

"Marry me, Rachel. Make me the happiest man alive and be my wife."

She started to cry. "Oh, Noah! I do love you."

"And?"

"I will marry you, if you are certain."

He realized hers were happy tears. "I have never been more certain in my life."

"Then, *ja,* I will marry you, Noah Lapp." It was as if the sun shone forth from her glistening brown eyes.

Noah laughed. "We can be married in November, the time for weddings. By then you will be well enough to stand by my side." He stood and came around to the other side of the bed. He leaned down and kissed her.

As their mouths touched, Rachel felt an overwhelming happiness. "I love you," she said when his head lifted. In answer, he kissed her again.

"And I love you," he said as he slowly straightened.

It was then that Rachel saw Katie Lapp in the doorway with Noah's milk shake in her hand. She blushed.

Noah noted Rachel's embarrassment and realized that someone had entered the room. *"Mam?"*

"*Ja,* Noah," Katie said, sweeping into the room to set Noah's milk shake on Rachel's bedside table. "I see you asked and got your answer."

Noah grinned at his mother. "*Ja.* She gave me the answer I'd hoped for."

Katie looked pleased. "It will be *gut* to have another daughter," she told Rachel.

Rachel beamed at her as she silently thanked the Lord for answering her prayers. "And it will be wonderful to belong to the Lapp family."

Epilogue

In early November, long after the fall harvest, the church community gathered together on a Tuesday in the home of the King family to celebrate the marriage of Noah Lapp and Rachel Hostetler. The occasion was a joyful affair, which promised to last from early morning until early evening for the elders; the young people would later head into the barn to continue the party well into the night. Rachel's family had come to Happiness from Millersburg, Ohio; Ezekiel and Henrietta Hostetler had been pleased to meet Rachel's intended and to witness firsthand their daughter's joy.

Noah and Rachel's intent to marry had been "published," or announced before the community, five weeks previously. Only a few close friends and neighbors had truly known about or suspected the couple's courtship. The seriousness of their relationship wasn't officially recognized until it was published.

The day he had taken Rachel to the hospital, Noah had been at Abram Peachy's house presenting to the deacon his desire to marry. Under normal circumstances, Abram would have gone to Rachel's family,

usually her parents, to inquire of the wishes of the prospective bride-to-be. Rachel's illness and hospital stay
had changed things. Under the circumstances, Noah had
been unable to hold back from asking Rachel to be his
wife, and everyone had understood.

In October, after Fast Day and on the day the Amish
take fall communion, Noah and Rachel requested proper
certifications of church membership. On the second
church Sunday after their request, Noah and Rachel
happily became members of the church, as was desired
and necessary in preparation for their union. The Sunday the banns were published, Rachel and Noah didn't
attend church service, but ate dinner together quietly
in Rachel's kitchen.

Usually a newly married couple would live with the
bride's parents, but not in this instance. After their marriage Noah and Rachel would live in the teacher's cottage until another house could be built for them on Lapp
land. Rachel would remain a teacher until then or a time
when a new teacher could be found to take her place.

After the couple vowed before all that their union
was ordained by God, there was singing and preaching
and finally all enjoyed food, seated in various places in
the house. Partition walls had been removed to unite
rooms and the guests. The bride and groom sat at the
Eck table in the most viewed corner of the Kings' extended living room. The bridal party sat with them, each
man or boy in the wedding party—in this case five of
Noah's brothers—was situated across the table from a
woman of his choosing. These men had escorted the
women to the table while holding their hands. Jedidiah
sat across from Annie Zook while Jacob chose Rachel's
cousin Nancy. Noah's brother Elijah finally enjoyed
his chance to spend time with Rebekka Miller. Daniel

and Isaac weren't inclined to choose partners, but as was custom at an Amish wedding, partners were chosen for them—Mary Hershberger for Daniel and Martha Mast for Isaac, and the two brothers did not object as they escorted the women to their chairs. Both girls were older than these Lapp brothers, but it didn't matter. The partnering was for celebration purposes only.

Seated with his new bride in the *Eck* corner, Noah turned to Rachel and drank his fill of her. There was a radiant smile on her face as she eyed the wedding guests. He saw she was particularly interested in watching her cousin Charlotte with her betrothed, Abram Peachy. The couple's intent to marry had been published only recently, and a December wedding was planned. Noah agreed that Charlotte had never looked happier. Abram's children loved her, as did their father, who couldn't keep his eyes off her.

As if sensing Noah's attention, Rachel slowly faced him.

"Rachel Lapp," he said with a smile.

She grinned, looking more relaxed and happy than he'd ever seen her. He knew he had helped to put that twinkle in her brown eyes and that upward curve to her pink lips. She wore her new navy-blue linen Sunday-best dress, sewn by her aunt for the occasion. Her white prayer *kapp* was also new, fashioned of white organdy in the Happiness community style, her apron and cape in matching white. She would wear the dress and *kapp* again come next church Sunday. The apron she would put away for her funeral someday.

"Noah, my husband," she murmured softly. Rachel studied him with love. He wore a suit sewn for him by his mother. Hooks and eyes secured his black coat and vest over his white shirt. Black pants were held up by suspenders under his vest. He had donned a black bow tie, which, she knew, felt unfamiliar to him, for this was the one occasion he would be allowed to wear one. Earlier, he had taken off his black wide-brimmed hat and hung it on a wall hook. Rachel could easily see his face, and she loved what she read in his expression.

She leaned close to whisper, "I love you."

He grinned. "As well you should, since you just declared so before the eyes of the Lord God and the members of our church."

She made a face and he easily slipped his hand around her back. He dipped his head to whisper in her ear. "I will love you forever, Rachel Lapp."

She shivered with pleasure at his breath in her ear, against her neck. "And I will love you forever, Noah." Then she took a quick glance to see that no one was watching at that very second, and she turned her head to plant a kiss on his cheek.

She leaned back in her chair. "I have truly found happiness in Lancaster County," she breathed softly.

"*We* have found true happiness together," Noah murmured, holding her close.

* * * * *

If you enjoyed this story by Rebecca Kertz,
be sure to check out the other books this month
from Love Inspired!

Dear Reader,

Welcome to Happiness, an Old Order Amish community in Lancaster County, Pennsylvania! Here you will meet the Amos Kings, the Samuel Lapps and other community members, including Rachel Hostetler, the new schoolteacher from Millersburg, Ohio. Rachel has left the safety of her parents' home to start anew after recuperating from a buggy accident that forever changed her life. Only two people know the true extent of Rachel's injuries—her aunt Mae King and Mae's closest friend, Katie Lapp. Noah Lapp, one of Katie's seven sons, first encounters Rachel when he saves the terrified young woman from a runaway buggy. Rachel, grateful for the rescue, learns that Noah is her cousin Charlotte's closest friend in her new Happiness community.

It is my pleasure to bring you Rachel and Noah's love story. It is a tale about new beginnings, about Amish family life and about real, hardworking people who live quietly and contentedly among us in this fast-paced, sometimes crazy world we live in.

The Lord gives us strength in times of great need. Rachel and Noah experience God's love and strength when they most need Him. I hope you enjoy their story, and that you believe, as I do, that God always has an alternate plan for us when our own goes awry.

I invite you to enter the world of the Lapps and the Kings. I hope you find joy in the journey.

Many blessings and much happiness,

Rebecca Kertz

Questions for Discussion

1. Why did Rachel come to Happiness, PA? Did you feel Rachel had courage for traveling so far from home? Do you think she made the right choice?

2. What is *rumspringa* and why do the elders of the church allow it?

3. Do you think Rachel really believed that Noah and her cousin Charlotte were meant to be together? If she did, why do you think she liked him? Can we help how we feel about someone?

4. Rachel found strength in the Lord, as did Noah. Can you recall some instances when Rachel and Noah asked for God's help? Can you list times in your life when God gave you comfort or strength?

5. After she learned that Noah wanted to court her, and not Charlotte, how did Rachel react? What worried her about getting involved with him once she knew that her cousin liked Abram Peachy?

6. Rachel finally agreed to allow Noah to court her. Considering her concerns regarding marriage, why did she agree? Do you think that she wanted to enjoy whatever time she could with him until he learned her secret fear?

7. Do you believe that Rachel hoped God would help her when she needed Him most? What happened in her past that had Rachel seeking and finding

strength from God? What lesson did she learn from the experience?

8. *The Budget* is the Amish newspaper from which Amish communities get news from others throughout the United States. One can read about everything from the births, illnesses, deaths and the conditions of one's farm or livestock, as well as anything else the Amish deem important or newsworthy. How important do you think this paper is for the Amish community and why?

9. When Abram's barn burned, members of his Amish community held a barn-raising to help him rebuild. Do you believe they did this because Abram was church deacon? Or would they help anyone in their community who needed them? Can you think of other instances that the Amish are there for each other? Do you find it inspiring? Are there ways you can help others in need in your own life?

10. Do you feel that Noah and Rachel will have a good marriage? What was it about Noah that made Rachel trust and believe that she could marry and find happiness with him?

REQUEST YOUR FREE BOOKS!

2 FREE INSPIRATIONAL NOVELS
PLUS 2
FREE
MYSTERY GIFTS

Love Inspired

YES! Please send me 2 FREE Love Inspired® novels and my 2 FREE mystery gifts (gifts are worth about $10). After receiving them, if I don't wish to receive any more books, I can return the shipping statement marked "cancel." If I don't cancel, I will receive 6 brand-new novels every month and be billed just $4.74 per book in the U.S. or $5.24 per book in Canada. That's a saving of at least 21% off the cover price. It's quite a bargain! Shipping and handling is just 50¢ per book in the U.S. and 75¢ per book in Canada.* I understand that accepting the 2 free books and gifts places me under no obligation to buy anything. I can always return a shipment and cancel at any time. Even if I never buy another book, the two free books and gifts are mine to keep forever.

105/305 IDN F47Y

Name _____ (PLEASE PRINT) _____

Address _____ Apt. # _____

City _____ State/Prov. _____ Zip/Postal Code _____

Signature (if under 18, a parent or guardian must sign)

Mail to the Harlequin® Reader Service:
IN U.S.A.: P.O. Box 1867, Buffalo, NY 14240-1867
IN CANADA: P.O. Box 609, Fort Erie, Ontario L2A 5X3

**Are you a subscriber to Love Inspired books
and want to receive the larger-print edition?
Call 1-800-873-8635 or visit www.ReaderService.com.**

* Terms and prices subject to change without notice. Prices do not include applicable taxes. Sales tax applicable in N.Y. Canadian residents will be charged applicable taxes. Offer not valid in Quebec. This offer is limited to one order per household. Not valid for current subscribers to Love Inspired books. All orders subject to credit approval. Credit or debit balances in a customer's account(s) may be offset by any other outstanding balance owed by or to the customer. Please allow 4 to 6 weeks for delivery. Offer available while quantities last.

Your Privacy—The Harlequin® Reader Service is committed to protecting your privacy. Our Privacy Policy is available online at www.ReaderService.com or upon request from the Harlequin Reader Service.

We make a portion of our mailing list available to reputable third parties that offer products we believe may interest you. If you prefer that we not exchange your name with third parties, or if you wish to clarify or modify your communication preferences, please visit us at www.ReaderService.com/consumerschoice or write to us at Harlequin Reader Service Preference Service, P.O. Box 9062, Buffalo, NY 14269. Include your complete name and address.

LI13R

He took up her whole office.

At least that's how it felt to Melissa Sweeney.

Brian Montclair sat in the chair across from her, his arms folded over his chest, his entire demeanor screaming "get me out of here."

Tall with broad shoulders and arms filling out his button-down shirt rolled up at the sleeves, he looked more like a linebacker than a potential baker's assistant.

Which is what he might become if he took the job Melissa had to offer him.

Melissa held up the worn and dog-eared paper she had been given. It held a short list of potential candidates for the job at her bakery.

The rest of the names had been crossed off with comments written beside them. Unsuitable. Too old. Unable to be on their feet all day. Just had a baby. Nut allergy. Moved away.

This last comment appeared beside two of the eight names on her list, a sad commentary on the state of the town of Bygones.

When Melissa had received word of a mysterious

benefactor offering potential business owners incentive money to start up a business in the small town of Bygones, Kansas, she had immediately applied. All her life she had dreamed of starting up her own bakery. She had taken courses in baking, decorating, business management, all with an eye to someday living out the faint dream of owning her own business.

When she had been approved, she'd quit her job in St. Louis, packed up her few belongings and had come here. She felt as if her life had finally taken a good turn. However, in the past couple of weeks it had become apparent that she needed extra help.

She had received the list of potential hires from the Bygones Save Our Street Committee and was told to try each of them. Brian Montclair was on the list. At the bottom, but still on the list.

"The reason I called you here was to offer you a job," she said, trying to inject a note of enthusiasm into her voice. This had better work.

To find out if Melissa and Brian can help save the town of Bygones one cupcake at a time, pick up
THE BACHELOR BAKER
wherever Love Inspired books are sold.

LIEXP0713

Love Inspired

CARING **Canines**

Both Abbey Harris and Dominic Winters long for a second chance at love, and it'll take two adorable dogs and a sweet little girl to bring them together.

Healing Hearts
by Margaret Daley

Available August 2013
wherever Love Inspired books are sold.